Immortality

The Enlightenment

Sophyath Pheng

VANTAGE PRESS
New York

This is a work of fiction. Any similarity between the names and characters in this book and any real persons, living or dead, is purely coincidental.

Cover design by Polly McQuillen

FIRST EDITION

Copyright © 2007 by Sophyath Pheng

Published by Vantage Press, Inc.
419 Park Ave. South, New York, NY 10016

Manufactured in the United States of America
ISBN: 978-0-533-15630-6

Library of Congress Catalog Card No.: 2006908543

0 9 8 7 6 5 4 3 2 1

I would like to dedicate this book to my beloved parents who have given me life and brought me into this world and taught me to live and love; and to my great family who've believed in me and my imagination.

I also would like to dedicate this book to everyone who has truly considered life and the living things surrounding him or her as the precious gifts from the greatest Creator of this Universe and who never gives up hope upon life when he or she experiences and journeys through the darkness or hardship.

Most of us wish life could be immortal when our Creator created our first ancestors on this planet, called Earth. We wish that all people could live peacefully with harmonies together in this world. For a period of time of our life, we should all live to enjoy life and share the world and the happiness with the others . . . and forget about the wars and hatred.

I believe somewhere out there, in the Universe, the immortality and the enlightenment existed, and then perhaps in our next lives, we will be there.

May our Creator bless and guide us through our journeys in these lives to reach the enlightenment and to make the world the better place for every generation and all of us.

Preface

Many thousands of years ago in cyberian history, legendary Warrior Aquarus, the greatest swordsman known to cyberkind as an honest man who always stood to defend the fairness and the truth of the good people from the evil, was on the quest in the search for the most extraordinary plant, called Oradius. With the magically energetic molecules, Oradius's fruits would sustain the youth of the cyberian body to stay young forever. The rareness of the supernatural power from these magic fruits could turn cyberian into the immortality with the mighty strength, the exceptional ability of a visionary to see the past or the future, and the supernatural intelligence close to God. As the great legend of these extraordinary fruits had scattered all over the kingdoms around the cyber planet, many of the kings, queens, priests, wizards, witches, and even the ordinary people wanted to have the taste of these mysterious fruits and to become an immortal kind. More and more cyber people endlessly explored and tried to find this secret plant; thus, they had never returned. Many years had passed by, most of the people had forgotten. Some of them tried to forget because no one could ever find this heavenly plant or they just believed it would never exist on this inexplicable planet. Again many generations later in the cyberian history, the rise of the Eastern and Western Civilization Dynasties, the Emperors and Empresses had ordered their people to adventurously explore for the precious plant and for those who sought for the plants, they also had never returned back to their homeland. Then, only the holy child who was pure at heart with greatest soul and who was chosen by the God of the Enlightenment to receive the greatest gift of life, immortality, would be brought to discover and receive the fruits of the eternal life to become the most powerful one very close to God and to serve his will.

1

Defeat of Optimus

Through the eyes of God looking upon the stars and the planets in the universe aiming at the mysterious and magical planet, the year was 390,000,000 A.U. (After the birth of the Universe) when Krometus, Krome for short, turned twelve years old. His father was a chief of a small village called Freewill, which was very far, far away from the Almar and all other kingdoms. Freewillian people peacefully lived in the evergreen hidden valley on the higher elevation region for many years although they were not the tribe people. They were from royal and noble families who sought for the freedom and the new way of life from all the corrupted societies. This hidden valley was remotely located in the middle of the tropical jungle that was not far from Mt. Aquarium. Freewill village was not ruled by any kingdom, the people were highly responsible and they lived happily together in the harmony as one small community. Mt. Aquarium was known as the highest mountain on the Cyber planet in the tropical mountain region. It was considered like a paradise and secret place where many of the magical treasures, plants, and creatures existed for many millions of years. Each child in the family had a special mark like a tattoo to identify which family he or she came from. Some fathers taught their young children to fish and hunt while other

1

adults harvested wild crops, plants, and fruits for their stock nearby the beautiful clear lake. The various sounds of the birds' songs echoed through the thickest evergreen giant trees as the monkeys endlessly jumped from tree to tree; Krome with the other two young hunters moved quietly closer to the wild beasts. He precisely aimed his bow and released the arrow at the heart of the animal. The arrow flew straight through the air and struck deep into the body of the wild boar as it ran and squealed. The big, male, wild boar became paralyzed with Krome's arrow as it struggled for a short distance before it fell down on the ground.

"It is a perfect shot, Krome. Your crossbow skill is wonderful," said his friends.

"Hold on! Don't get too close to animal yet." Krome stopped his friends.

"Why not, Krome? " his friend asked.

"He might hurt you back if he is still alive . . . please make sure he is dead before you touch him . . . let me give it another shot," Krome told his friend as he shot another arrow at the animal before they got close and touched it.

"I think he is dead now, Krome . . . see, he is not moving," one of his friends said.

"Let remove its testicles and bring this animal back to our village before it spoils," Krome said to his friends. They hurriedly cut off the testicles before it spread its hormone into the entire body and brought the dead wild boar back to their village.

Most men in Freewill were the great swordsmen and archers. They passed on these skills to their young to protect the village and their families from all harm and intruders. The next day Krome and his younger brother, Protus, were excited to learn the new skill of the fighting sword from their father, Optimus.

"Krome and Protus, this is not play. You have to pay very close attention to me. Because this is a useful skill for you to learn to protect yourself, your family and your people . . . especially you, Krome . . . you must learn this skill," Optimus said to his sons.

"Yes, Father, please forgive me . . . Protus stop bordering me!" Krome said.

"Don't just stand there, come here, Krome, and hold this sword up and point to that direction. I know that it is a little bit heavy for you but you must learn to build up your muscles and your strength, Son," Optimus said.

"First you slash down to your lower left, second back up to your right and then swing around to your upper left." Optimus showed Krome his moves. Krome seemed to be a little weak and lost his control; he almost slashed his father's face.

"Krome, you have to be careful and take it easy. You do not have to jump too far from your first position. You only move your steps back and forth like this." Optimus suddenly jumped back and explained by showing Krome again all of his moves.

"Sorry . . . Father, I will try my best again," Krome said.

Krome became better and continued the practice with his sword lesson for the day.

"Protus, you have to watch your brother and me. I think that you are too small to hold this sword. When you grow up I will let you learn like your brother and here is the stick, you can pretend it is your sword," Optimus turned around to Protus and said softly as he did not want Protus to be disappointed.

"Hah, hah, hah, hah . . . Mother look at me!" Protus laughed and said.

He took the stick from his father and he ran with maneuverable action as a child at play, jumped up and down to show his mother, Merida.

The sun was almost over the mountain and a man named Rima rode a horse toward Optimus; he invited him to go hunting on the other side of the mountains.

"Chief Optimus, are you going to hunt with us today?" Rima asked.

"No, Rima, I have decided to stay with my sons and will train them the sword lesson. Please could you bring these arrows and give them to my brother, Colisus. Tell him to be careful; do not go down too far from the mountains because we do not want the outsiders to find this place. And remember never kill or harm the unicorns," Optimus told the man.

"Yes, Chief, I will forward your brother these words," Rima said.

Rima took the arrows from Optimus and turned his horse around then he rode to join his group. Optimus stood worriedly as he watched all his men ride the horse through the passage of the mountains. He seemed to know something would happen to his people as he uncertainly imagined how long this hideout would be last from Valimus's probe.

"I hope Valimus's people will never find out this valley. This will be the last battle ground for me and him if he ever comes here," Optimus whispered in his mind.

In Almar Kingdom, Diron, the evil wizard who dedicated himself and worshiped to the God of Darkness to gain the dark power, wanted to take control over cyberian minds to follow his destiny, the force of darkness. Once every year he got together with other evil wizards from many other kingdoms at a secret place, a mountain called Soulless Mountain, to perform a ritual sacrifice to gain the magical powers and the extension of their cyberian lives. In the ring of the sacrifice they combined their powers to seek for a holy child who would become an immortal warrior and would lead to fight against the darkness. They were also seeking for the secret animals to use in their sacrifice. With the help from the power of the God of Darkness, they were able to see a child in a remote valley in the middle of the jungles who would rise with the mighty power and would be able to destroy them. The child would weaken the power of the God of Darkness. They had found the secret place where the holy child lived and they both had agreed to make a plan to kill the child. Diron, the leader of the Circle of Darkness, made a decision with the other evil Wizards to use all his power to go after the holy child.

Princess Hollidia was very sick under the spell of the evil wizard, Diron, who served her father's kingdom. Diron used his evil magic to gain and sustain his power in Almar Kingdom as the highest Wizard. Beside Diron, the king's Head of the Armies, Lord Valimus was also an evil man who used his power to suppress the citizens of Almar Kingdom. Valimus had betrayed Optimus after he took control over the armies in the Kingdom. He became very obsessive with Merida's charm. She was already in love and was engaged to Optimus. Optimus and Merida secretly escaped along with other followers after they had learned Valimus's deadly plan. Besides that conflict, Optimus had studied the legend of Warrior Aquarus and his magic sword so he decided to leave the kingdom to search for the mighty sword. They all mysteriously disappeared into the tropical jungles without a trace. Valimus had spent more than a decade to find Merida and Optimus; he still had no idea where these people had been hiding. He was ambiguous as he had never given up the search. Diron needed to capture and sacrifice the holy child with the blood from a silver horn unicorn to protect the God of Darkness and to increase his magical power and his life extension. Valimus wanted to go on searching for Merida and to kill Optimus. They both discussed and found their final solutions then Diron put his evil spell on the little Princess Hollidia. They secretly agreed to convince King Hemiro; therefore, they could use the king's soldiers to capture the holy child, the silver horn unicorn and to search for Optimus's existence. King Hemiro asked the highest Wizard what reason caused his daughter to fall into a mysterious sickness and what action or medicine could be used to save his daughter's life.

"Wizard Diron, could you use your wizard power to determine the cause of my beloved daughter's illness? It seems so strange to me," the King asked.

"Your majesty, Princess Hollidia is sick by a very angry spirit . . . we need to sacrifice the life of the silver horn unicorn to our Divine then he will forgive the little princess and spare her life from the darkness," Diron explained to the king.

"Wizard Diron, where could we find this secret animal?" King Hemiro asked.

"Your majesty, these animals are living in the Aquarium Mountains region. It is located far across the ocean to the southwest of our kingdom. To reach there, it might take three months but Princess Hollidia will live until the next five hundred days according to my elemental calculation," Diron explained to the king.

King Hemiro hurriedly ordered Lord Valimus to assemble his armies and supplies to explore the Aquarium Mountain region to capture a silver horn unicorn for the sacrifice to save the life of his only daughter.

"Lord Valimus, I order you to assemble your armies and supplies to immediately explore the Aquarium

Mountain region and you must capture the silver horn unicorn to save my daughter's life. In the return of your success, I will reward you with more gold, lands and servants . . . and of course your power," the king ordered.

"Your majesty, I will find the silver horn unicorn and we will return soon because of Princess Hollidia must be saved from this sickness," Valimus submissively replied.

"Lord Valimus, do you know that the Aquarium Mountain region does not belong to our kingdom? The legend had been told that many cybermen had disappeared into those mysterious jungles. I will give you more armies than you will ever need; in case if any resistances obstruct your destiny," the King continued.

"Your majesty, I humbly appreciate for your brilliant vision and intellectuality. We will be able to capture the secret animal as we promise to save Princess Hollidia from her mysteriously chronic illness, my king," Valimus and Diron replied to the King.

Valimus called all his strong men to assemble large armies and prepare more supplies at once. He personally commanded the group of the armies on this exploration. They had traveled many days from northeast to southwest across the mountains and ocean toward the other Hemisphere. They moved from green pine, oak jungles to the Great Plains. The weather got hotter as they passed through the great plain desert. A week across the desert, they had reached the Cactus plantation. There was a little town nearby the big lake. Valimus ordered his soldiers to occupy the little town for a few days. Valimus was an evil man and many of his soldiers were barbarians. They forced the people to prepare food and serve them as their own slaves. They even abused some of the young women to have fun with them. They left the little town the next morning and kept moving to the southwest direction.

They started to see the highest top of Aquarium Mountain from very far away after they had traveled many days across the rocky ground. The sun almost set as they reached higher ground with many green bushes. Valimus stopped his horse and looked around then he ordered his armies to camp out for the night. They did not realize this region was full of poisonous snakes during nighttime.

Suddenly, the strong sounds of the men cried out in pain from the snake bites and one of the soldiers ran to the front of Valimus's tent and informed him about the incident.

"My lord, this area is full of snakes; we should inform all of our soldiers to take the precaution. I got the report that twelve men have been bitten by these poisonous snakes and Wizard Diron would not able to save them, my lord . . . what should we do?" One of the soldiers ran to the front of the tent to report the incident to Valimus.

"General, sound the horn and tell them to get rid of these snakes," Valimus ordered.

"Yes, my lord . . . I will tell our men at once," the soldier answered.

Diron helped by using his wizard power to chase the snakes away; through the night soldiers stayed awake and fought with the snakes. The sky was lighted up with red color on the horizon in the early dawn. Valimus had ordered his armies to rest for a few more hours as the snakes went back to their holes.

"Wizard Diron, twelve of our soldiers just died from the snake bites. I just can't believe this could happen," Valimus told Diron with his anger.

"Lord Valimus, if I had the blood from the silver horn unicorn, my magical power would be able to sense all these dangers," Diron regrettably replied.

A few hours later Valimus ordered one of his knights

to tell the soldier to get ready to move on and to watch out for the other dangers.

"General Maxus, you must order our armies to move out at once. Tell them to keep their eyes open and be ready at all times; this is the legend come to life," Valimus warned.

"Yes, my lord, they are aware of these dangers," General Maxus said.

They passed through the green fields and they had reached the edge of the jungles. They moved through the creepy jungles along the swamps toward Aquarium Mountain. The two soldiers went into the trees to release their internal wastes next to swamps and they kept their eyes wide open as they looked around for the wild creatures but they did not realize that the smell of their wastes drew the attention of the wild animals.

"You are a bitch, your smell is very bad . . . what did you eat this morning? It looks like you have a rotten stomach . . . damn you," one of them complained to the other.

"Heh, heh . . . your smell is worse than mine . . . just finish it faster or the crocs might come up and get your stupid ass . . . heh, heh," the other said back.

They both did not know that beneath the swamps was a big snake moving closer to them and ready to come up to the surface to taste their cyberian flesh and with a blink of the eyes one of them was constrained by the snake and died instantly without a sound from his mouth. The sound of crushing bones made the other turn around and looked at his partner, he became speechless and paralyzed as he tried to escape for his life. The big snake released the other soldier down on the ground and went very fast after the other one. The snake constrained and devoured the second man and then the dead one on the ground and went back into the swamps.

They battled with another giant snake on the following day; they had lost a few more men before the snake went away. The next night, a few of the soldiers were eaten by the big black mountain lions. They grew more scared as they had experienced and had seen all these incidents as their trips brought them closer to the Aquarium Mountains region.

In Freewill, Merida had a bad dream in the middle of the night. She called out her husband's name as she moved helplessly in her sleep. Optimus was suddenly awakened by his wife's nightmare and reached out to wake her up.

"Wake up, Merida," said Optimus, "please wake up! What's bothering you?"

Merida woke up with her hands shaking as she was in the state of intense fear.

"What is it disturbing you, Merida? Please tell me," Optimus asked.

"Please you can tell me, I'm here, my dear," Optimus comforted his wife.

"I had a bad dream . . . that Valimus and his armies discovered and burned our village. They killed all our men including you. I'm very scared, Optimus," Merida said.

"My dear, we have escaped for almost fourteen years. They could never find us. I believe; they will never find out about this place. Even if they find us here; I will fight to protect you, our children and our people," Optimus calmed down his wife and said.

Optimus held his wife tighter as he spoke with her. Meridia rested on Optimus's body then she turned her head around to watch her sons in their sleep. She reached out her right hand to touch the boys' hair and whispered to Optimus.

"Optimus, I am still very frightened. It was so real in my dream. I just can't close my eyes with this terrifying image . . . I think we should find other place," Merida said.

"It is just a bad dream. Please do not be afraid . . . my darling," Optimus said.

Optimus kissed Merida's head as he tried to reassure his wife's worriment. A few hours later she had fallen back into her sleep on his chest. He carefully lifted her body to the other side of the wooden bed and walked out of the cottage quietly. The night weather was a little bit cooler; the light of the full moon shined upon the Aquarium and the clear lake was magnificent. Optimus stood silently and took a deep breath in this peaceful night as he whispered to himself.

"I wish this peaceful moment will exist upon this valley forever. Mighty God, please help me to protect my people and this valley from the evil forces. I have asked you many times and please hear my voice one more time," Optimus said.

Optimus and his people did not realize that now Valimus's armies had reached the skirt of the Aquarium. It only took them one more day to reach their village. The next morning had arrived; Valimus's armies had spotted the horse footprints of Optimus's hunting group. Valimus ordered some of his armies to spy and follow the trace of these horses. They hid out in the jungle and waited to find out who these people were. People in the Freewill village woke up and performed their routine work as usual. Most of the men including Optimus went down the mountain to hunt but this time they did not go far from the mountains. However, they were still spotted by Valimus's soldiers and they were secretly followed back to their village. The soldiers went back to inform Valimus about the location of the village. Valimus was a smart man when it came to face with the battle and his enemies; he had many great experiences of how to defeat his opponents. He ordered his armies to move quietly to surround the Freewill village during night time and surprisingly attacked them by day.

As the sun lighted up the sky on the following day, the voices of Valimus's armies shouted out very loud from all directions toward Freewill village. Valimus ordered his soldiers to kill all men in the village and capture all the women and the children.

"Merida . . . hurry! You must take the horses and our sons to escape to the mountains and wait for me over there . . . you must go now!" Optimus told his wife.

"Krome, be careful; you must go because you have a great responsibility to take good care of your mother and your brother if I won't make it . . . do you hear me, Krome? You both must leave now . . . hurry! Go!!!" Optimus spoke to his son.

"Optimus, may God protect you and our men . . . please take good care yourself . . . I'll wait for you on other side of that mountain," Merida told her husband.

Optimus boldly drew his long sword and ran toward his enemies as he shouted to tell all his men to be brave to fight against Valimus's armies.

"We must fight to defend our families and our freedom! The evil man like him shall never rule over people like us!" Optimus said.

Krome rode on one horse while Merida and Protus rode on another. They both headed into the jungles but they were chased by Valimus's knights. The great force of Optimus's sword slashed through Valimus's soldiers' bodies one by one and each swing Optimus's blade took the soul of each soldier. Valimus then used his skillful archers to defeat all Freewillian warriors. All Optimus's men were the great sword warriors but they were outnumbered by Valimus's armies. Optimus fell down on his knees as an arrow hit and impaled his body. He was holding on to his sword as he struggled and tried to stand up with the blood from his chest. He stood up again but Valimus rode the horse toward him. Valimus swung his sword and slashed through Optimus's throat; Optimus fell down on his back for the last time. Valimus turned his horse around and looked over Optimus's body just to make sure he was dead.

Merida shouted to Krome with panic when she saw Valimus's soldiers were chasing behind her closer and closer.

"Krome, faster, hurry, you must go . . . go!!!" Merida told Krome.

Valimus's knights almost caught up with her. In a moment, Krome felt like he wanted to turn around to help his mother and his brother but Merida kept shouting to him not to turn back as Valimus's soldiers approached her.

"Krome, you must escape. They will kill you . . . faster . . . you must go!!!" Merida said.

"Mother, you must hurry, hurry, Mother . . . come on!" Krome called his mother.

Krome turned his head back to see his mother. Too late, Valimus's knights already surrounded Meridia and Protus as her horse halted to a complete stop a distance away behind him. Krome rode his horse faster as one of Valimus's knights still chased after him onto the mountains. Suddenly Krome approached a dead-end path and he quickly jumped off from the horseback. In front of him, it was a very deep cliff and he could not even see the bottom of it. He looked around trying to find the way to cross to the other side of the mountain but he saw only the branch of a huge tree grown over the cliff. Krome ran toward the tree then he began to climb onto the branch as Valimus's knight got off the horseback walking toward the tree. Krome still heard his mother's words inside his head. "Krome you must escape. They will kill you . . . you must go!!!" He was very frightened while he crawled along on the big branch of the tree over the cliff. It started to get harder as Krome reached near the end because the green wet mosses that were growing on the tree were slippery and too hard to hang onto the branch. Krome shakily moved his hand to reach out for a small branch as he felt slippery and unfortunately it was a dead branch. The snapping sound of the small dead branch echoed over the cliff as Krome's body completely fell off the branch. For the last time Krome desperately shouted out loud when his body freely fell into the fogs near the half way down along the cliff formation.

"Father . . . please, help me . . . somebody help me!!!" Krome called for help.

"Nobody will ever survive in this fall. Too deep, and too bad I only wanted to capture you, jungle boy," the soldier said.

Valimus's knight whispered to himself and took Krome's horse back to the village.

"My lord, the boy is dead. He fell down to the bottom of the cliff," the knight said.

"No, no . . . not Krome . . . not Krome . . . my son!" Merida cried out.

Her face was full with tears and grief as she looked around trying to find the body of her husband. She suddenly fell down on her knees and mourned over Optimus's body.

"My beloved Optimus . . . it cannot be . . . oh God,

14

why, why? Optimus why? Optimus, Krome . . . Oh Krome, my beloved son," Merida cried with her grief.

Valimus got down from the back of his horse and walked straight to Merida. He spoke and laughed excitingly as he saw Optimus's dead body lay down on the ground.

"Well, well, well . . . after all these years, I finally have found my charming lady. . . . Hah, hah, ha, hah, hah," Valimus said and laughed.

Merida got up and walked toward Valimus. She raised her head up then she spit on Valimus's face. She fought violently and desperately against him.

"You, murderer, I hope . . . I will take your life," Merida said.

She was held back by his soldiers as Protus ran toward her and held on to her leg.

"Please don't hurt my mother . . . please let her go!" Protus begged.

Protus was pushed down to the ground and he looked at Optimus's body lying on the ground which was stuck with many arrows on his chest. He tried to hold on tight to his mother's legs but Valimus's soldiers pulled him away from her.

Valimus had lost almost half of his armies in this bloody battle; he had defeated Optimus at last. He ordered his soldiers to capture the rest of the women and children. Diron, with some of soldiers on other side of the lake, were chasing after the silver horn unicorn into the water; they finally had captured the unicorn. Diron was very excited as he looked at the silver horn unicorn inside the cage. He ordered the soldiers to get back to the Freewill village but Diron was unable to tell which child was a holy child.

"I finally have eliminated my enemy and found the

woman who I have loved for many years. She has not changed for all these years. Wizard Diron, you also have captured your secret animal and these children are yours. We must go back to Almar Kingdom at once tomorrow before the king finds out," Valimus told Diron.

"Lord Valimus, your plan worked very well. We will find out which one is the holy child. I have heard that one boy just fell off from the cliff; he must be dead by now. We must be careful with the king," Diron replied.

Valimus ordered his armies to celebrate their victory and had a good time for their bloody battle at Freewill. They were joyful over the defeat of Optimus as they ran after the children and women. Some of them chased the women around; the others sat down in a circle and ate the barbecued wild animals. They were drunk in the feast of their victory. In that night Valimus's armies were scared to death as they were endlessly haunted and attacked by many wild beasts and the giant snakes. The creepy, unseen force haunted many soldiers, even Valimus and Diron; thus, more soldiers killed each other in the mysterious night. They thought the spiritual guardian of the village cursed them and they had decided to leave at once the next morning.

2

Krome's Survival

Krome lost consciousness as his body fell down through the fog along the cliff formation. The giant zygodactyl's feet suddenly swooped up his body before it hit the bottom of the cliff. The giant bird just secured its feet on both of Krome's arms next to his shoulders like its prey. The bird lifted Krome's body higher into the air in a slow motion as it tried to fly up toward the top of the mountain. The bird had flown for a while far higher from the place where Krome just fell down. He was still unconscious as the giant golden eagle looked down upon the mountainside to find a safe place for landing. Krome's body was a little bit heavy for the bird to carry all the way up to the top; it decided to land on the open spot of the mountainside. The giant eagle slowly released Krome's body down on the big rock with both of its wings swung up in the air. The bird used its huge beak to turn Krome's body around so it could see his face.

The bird calmly picked and cleaned its feet while it stood by Krome's body to wait for his awakening. Krome slowly moved his right arm as he weakly whispered in his half consciousness "Father . . . Please, help me!!!" He started to open his eyes but he fell back into unconsciousness as he saw the giant bird stood next to him. He felt very tired from the escape and he was thirsty. The giant bird suddenly took off and dived down into the cliff passing through the thick fogs. It reached the bottom of the cliff and landed on the big rock in the middle of the stream. The bird dipped its beak into the water then it lifted its head back up into the air. The giant bird repeated this movement for a few times before it took off from the rock flying up back onto the place where Krome was still unconscious. Now the giant eagle lowered its beak close to Krome's face and spit out the water from the stream into his mouth. Krome swallowed the water as he began to open his eyes again. He was very scared when he saw the giant bird for the second time. He yelled out loud as he tried to get up quickly. "Ah . . . help me . . . Father . . . help me!!!" The bird was very surprised by Krome's reaction; it almost fell back off from the big rock. Krome jumped off the rock; he began to run away from the giant bird. He turned his head back to see if the bird would chase after him. The bird stood placidly and watched his panic moves. Krome turned around to take a good look at the bird again; he realized it seemed to be a harmless creature.

He thought back over what had happened to him. He remembered a moment ago, he fell off the branch of the tree. Why had he landed on the rock without getting any cuts, bruises, or broken bones? He curiously looked up to the other side of the mountain and he looked at his body. "Hum . . . I would be getting wet if I had fallen into the water." He finally concluded that he was probably saved by this giant golden eagle. He carefully walked closer to the rock and he climbed back up on it to get near the bird. The bird did not make any move from the place it stood on. It only kept its eye contact with Krome. He lured the bird as he slowly raised his right hand to touch its feathers. The bird rapidly moved its head back and Krome quickly moved backward a few steps as he still felt unsafe. He gave himself one more try to pet the bird's chest; he succeeded his tempting. The bird pushed its head down gently against Krome's chest; they both became friends. Krome felt much better after all these bad things happened to him. He jumped off the big rock again. He looked around trying to find the path to go back down but there was no way down because it was too steep, very straight down. He looked up; he saw the slope was not too bad to climb so he started climbing up to the higher place.

Krome had been climbing up the mountainside more than half of the day but he still could not see the top of this gigantic mountain. He became very exhausted as the sun had almost set. He was very hungry; he searched around to see if any fruits or plants could be edible. Then he saw some green young leaves were grown next to the rock, it looked familiar, like the plant that his mother used to pick for him and his brother. He reached out to pick up a few leaves to put into his mouth. "This is good. It is so sweet. This would help to stop me from my thirst and hunger for tonight." Krome began to look around for the spot on the rock to sleep for the night after he fed up himself with the sweet leaves. As he began to fall into his sleep, the giant eagle flew down to rest by his side. The night was chilly but the feathers of the giant bird kept Krome very cozy. He slept well through the night from his exhausted body. From this height, the view was spectacular and the breeze was so pure with the fresh smell of the Aquarium atmosphere.

The stars were so bright in the first night after the full moon. The sound of the light wind swept by the mountainside was delightful. The giant bird and Krome sounded asleep peaceful; they both looked like the dead creatures on the rock. The early dawn was even more

19

striking if one viewed down from the rock where Krome and the giant eagle slept on. To watch the sun rising from this high altitude was breathtaking grandeur as the sky lighted up with the dark red and slowly transformed into the bright red on the far away horizon. Now the sun completely moved up from the edge of the planet, Krome had awakened and he started to talk to the giant bird.

"Big Bird, thank you for saving my life and stay by my side," Krome said.

He stood up and gave the giant bird a big hug. The bird gently petted its head back against Krome's body. They had become very close just for over the night. Krome sat back; he leaned his body against the giant eagle as he looked upon the sunrise, worrying about his family. He stood up to stretch his body and he spoke to the bird again.

"Big Bird, I think that I have to keep climbing to the top. Maybe I'll find the way down on the other side of this mountain. If I can't find the way back to my village, I'll die on this mountain alone. . . . My parents will probably look for me and I would like to know what would happen to my people at the Freewill Valley, especially my father. I must get to the top of this mountain and find my way back home," Krome said.

3

Discovery of the Magic Sword

Krome continued to climb for almost another half day; he still did not reach the top of the mountain. The giant bird flew up higher away from Krome and it gave him a sounding signal "Kwark! Kwark!" as it tried to land on the huge rock about a hundred yards up above him. He looked up to the bird and climbed faster toward the rock. He reached the top of the rock; he gratefully said to the bird, "Thank you! Big Bird, this is what I'm looking for" as he ran toward the middle of the rock. The rock had a shape like a small pool, which was able to hold a large volume of water from the rain. Krome kneeled down beside the water and he drank from it. He scooped the water with both hands to wash the dirt off his face and his body. He again spoke to the bird. "This feels so cool. . . . Don't you, Big Bird? I think that we are going to stay here for tonight," he drank some more water. He stood up looking to the other side of the rock; he saw a cyberian skeleton lying against the rock next to a long sword. He was afraid for a moment but he decided to go to take a closer look at the bones.

Krome quickly jumped off the rock and walked toward the skeleton. He stepped around wondering what had happened to this big man; he saw the dagger next to the waist of the skeleton. He reached down to pick it up and saw the gold necklace with big green pendant stone.

He picked both of the things up. He held the dagger in one hand as he turned it around to examine it. Then he stepped to the right side of skeleton toward the sword. He put down the dagger and the gold necklace. He bent his body down trying to lift the sword but he could not even move it off from the ground at all. He changed the spot to get his feet in the right position. He moved his both arms and shoulders back and forth; he tried to build the strength in his muscles to lift the sword one more time. Krome was amazed with the weight of the sword because he was still not able to move it at all. He gave up and he ran back to the rock as he called the giant bird.

"Look . . . look! What I have found, Big Bird," Krome shouted.

He lifted the dagger and the gold necklace to show the bird. Krome was so happy for a moment. He kept looking at both of the items while he lay down on the rock next to the water and the bird.

"I guess; we are very lucky, Big Bird . . . I mean myself . . . again thank you, Big Bird for saving my life from the fall," Krome said.

The bird took off from rock and flew up along the mountainside. He asked the bird to come back but the giant bird ignored him and kept flying away from him.

"Big Bird, where are you going? Please . . . come back!" Krome said to the bird.

Krome decided to rest on the rock for the day. The bird disappeared for many hours. He wondered perhaps the giant bird decided to leave him behind. A moment later, the bird flew back down with the cluster of the strange fruits and put them down next to Krome. The fruits resembled with the rainbow colors and released a fragrance lighter than the smell of the jasmine flower. Krome grew hungrier when he saw and smelled the fruits. It looked delightful for the appetite and Krome started to feel watery in his mouth. The bird made the sign by nodding its head up and down; it tried to explain to Krome that the fruits were safe to eat. He soon was able to understand the bird and he began to consume the fruits. Krome ate one by one until he had finished them all. He walked toward the water to wash his mouth and to have a drink. Because he was very hungry, he did not really taste the fruits. He slightly recognized that the fruits had no taste at all. Suddenly Krome felt dizzy and contracting all over his muscles. Then he began to feel very heavy in his head and his vision became blurry. He became like a paralyzed person; he decided to lie down next to the bird. Not for long, he completely fell into the unconscious state. By now he looked very much like a dead person after he ate all those strange fruits. Then he stopped breathing with his eyes opened.

The darkness started to take over the world as the sun completely disappeared from the sky. Night turned to day and day turned to night. Six days had passed by but Krome still did not wake up. Later on the sixth day he was able to move his head a little bit; he was dreaming as he had softly spoken in his sleep.

"Father . . . I have found some things. Here is the dagger and this is the gold necklace. Can I keep the dagger?" Krome whispered in his sleep.

"Yes, you can have them both . . . these things are yours because you found them. But Son, you must reach the top of this mountain and when you do, you must go to Almar Kingdom to save your mother and your brother," Optimus said in Krome's dream.

Krome saw his father jump off the rock and walk toward the sword beside the skeleton. He brought the sword back and gave it to him.

23

"This sword also belongs to you. You must take good care of this sword. I will see you later. Now I have to go, Son," Optimus again spoke in Krome's dream.

Krome saw his father reach down and kiss him on his head. Then he left him and disappeared into the trees.

"Father, wait for me. Please wait for me. Please don't go," Krome spoke louder and louder in his dream. "Father, please wait for me!"

He suddenly woke up; he realized that it was only a dream. He looked up to the sky and he talked to himself.

"I promise . . . I will find you. I'll find Mother and Protus too," Krome said.

It was the early morning as Krome sat up trying to remember what had happened to him. As he closed his eyes, he could see his father's body down near the lake with other people and his village was burned down. Krome quickly opened his eyes; he was very astonished. He could not believe himself because this was so real. He closed his eyes again then he saw his mother and his younger brother were traveling along with Valimus's armies across the desert.

"This cannot be real . . . or am I dreaming? No, I am awake," Krome thought.

Every moment he closed his eyes, he kept on seeing more things. As his visionary grew strong, he felt the strength in his body was increasing unusually. He looked at his body; he knew that his body had grown much taller and more muscular. His kilt was too small to fit him and he used the dagger to cut it loose. He retied his kilt back around his waist. He stretched his body; he felt like he could lift the big piece of rock near the water. Krome gave himself a try and he easily lifted the rock like the mighty Hercules without using even half of his strength. He felt very surprised as he put the rock down. Krome happily jumped around and with each jump, he could jump higher and higher almost to the top of the big tree.

"Big Bird . . . do you see? I am very strong . . . I can fly . . . I can fly," he said.

He lifted his body into the air like a bird and landed next to the giant golden eagle. He proudly gave the bird a big hug and he told the bird.

"Thank you, Big Bird . . . I think that must be the fruits. . . . It must be the fruits that you gave me, it has so much energies," Krome thanked and said to the bird.

By looking straight into the bird's eyes, he was able to understand the bird's mind; he knew that the bird agreed with him. Krome turned around and jumped off the rock. He walked to the sword by the skeleton; he bent down to pick the sword up again. He was able to lift it up this time but he still felt it a little bit heavy. He held the sword with his two hands; he swung it back and forth. The longer he practiced with the sword; he felt the sword got lighter. He took the sword and jumped back on the rock. Krome learned all his father's moves. He now could even hold the sword with just one hand; he threw the sword up high into the air then he jumped to catch it. Krome recognized that his strength was growing stronger; he felt his body lighter each time he jumped up.

"I will reach the top of this mountain today . . . please let's go . . . Big Bird," Krome said.

Krome tied the sword by his waist next to the dagger and he put the necklace around his neck. He jumped up from rock to rock like a monkey as the bird flew up along with him. He began to run up against the slope of the mountain like an eagle flying over the surface of the water. Krome moved upward side by side with the giant bird's speed.

"Faster, faster Big Bird . . . faster. . . . Hah, hah, hah, hah," Krome said and laughed.

Krome laughed and talked to the bird as he began to pass the bird behind. He had been running up the slope almost half of the day but he did not even feel tired at all. The bird finally had decided to take a rest as it landed on a rock below him. Krome stopped and he talked to the bird.

"What happened, Big Bird? Are you tired? Oh . . . well, we will take a rest here for a while. I feel so great; I feel like I can fly . . . again, thanks to you," Krome said to the bird.

He looked up to the top of the mountain; he saw it not far up from the place he sat. Krome took off again and he kept jumping from rock to rock until he reached the top. The giant eagle landed on the big rock next to him. He looked half way down from the top of the mountain, all he could see was clouds. Krome felt like he was in heaven as he stood to take a deep breath on the top of the giant mountain.

"Finally we have made it, Big Bird. It is very awesome up here. Look down from here . . . we can see the whole planet," Krome said.

He said to the giant eagle as it lifted its both wings up into the air. The bird relaxed and used its beak to clean and straighten its feathers. Krome still stood up astonishingly and looked around down very far distance upon these endless splendid views because he had never seen or been up on the highest place like this in his entire life.

The top of the Aquarium Mountain was so huge and long and was filled with the various beautiful plants, giant tropical trees blending with big stones and strange, natural spring water which ran down from the rock into a big pond. Many huge trees grew over the rocks with their roots attaching in different directions; they resembled the shape of swimming starfishes or octopuses. Krome turned around to look at the entire area; he was fascinatingly absorbed in the heavenly appearance of nature on the top of this greatest mountain. One spot was surrounded by the green medium mangrove trees like a circle a distance far away from where Krome was standing. Many striking flowers grew around the pond and aquatic plants flourished under crystal clear water as it tried to show their enchanted lives in this heavenly place. Krome lived in the tropical jungles and mountains all his childhood but he had never seen something close to this magnitude. Not far from his valley, Krome still had never seen the top of this mountain; he saw only the clouds that always surrounded it nearly halfway from the top.

4

Krome Meets Aquarus

Krome sat down on the rock and took a deep breath to taste the pure air, the fresh scent of the Aquarium as he closed his eyes. Suddenly a big, strong, muscular man with white hair and beard appeared in his vision and congratulated him.

"Krome, congratulations for your accomplishment, my name is Aquarus. The sword, dagger, and necklace that you have found belong to me. But I will give them all to you as the gifts of honor, you deserve to possess these things," Aquarus explained.

"Aquarus? I've heard your name before. You're the greatest swordsman who was on the quest to search for the Oradius plant for the King," Krome said to Aquarus.

"Yes, you're right. I had been searching for this magic plant for almost my entire life but I still couldn't find it. Thousands of years ago, I had traveled across many kingdoms, oceans, mountains and the jungles to seek for the plant then my life had ended up here. The place where you have found my sword was the place I last breathed. I got wounded from the battle and was very sick when I reached that big rock with one of my pet, golden eagles. I had almost reached the top of this mountain. I came very close . . . to find that precious plant which could turn my cyberian body into immortality," Aquarus said.

"I had battled with the giant snakes, lions, gorillas and the blue dragon before I reached the height of this mountainside. I got injured very badly after I defeated the blue dragon near the bottom of the mountain." Aquarus continued.

"But where is the Oradius plant? If you said that you came very close to finding it," said Krome, "perhaps it is here somewhere on this mountain."

"The six fruits which you just ate six days ago are the fruits of the Oradius, the fruits of the eternal life," Aquarus told Krome.

"The giant golden eagle that saved you from the fall, also belongs to me. His name is Aerian. Shortly after I had passed away, the eagle discovered and ate the fruits of the Oradius. He became the immortal bird and he has grown into a huge bird. Thus, he has never left this place since the day he ate the fruits. He has been living up here with my soul for many thousands of years."

Krome opened his eyes and looked at the giant golden eagle. He smiled and walked closer to the bird. He gently petted the neck of the giant eagle, looking straight into the eagle's eyes; he tried to use his inner spiritual power to communicate with the bird's mind. After it blinked its eyes, the bird took off and flew low toward the middle of the circle of the mangrove trees. Krome lifted his body into the air as he moved from rock to rock following the eagle. The bird now landed on the small rocky island next to the very strange-looking plants in the middle of the large pond. The water inside the pond was crystal clear; Krome could even see all green plants and the deepness of the pond. He decided to jump over the water to the rocky island; suddenly the two golden-green water dragons jumped out of the water flying toward him. He used his power to lift his body higher into the air as the two dragons landed on the spot where he had stood. They both aggressively flew upward to attack Krome. He seemed to recognize his flying capability as he floated into the air higher, avoiding the contact with the two dragons.

For a moment Krome thought that he should use his sword to defeat the two dragons. Then he clearly remembered his ability to use his inner spiritual power to influence the animal's mind, he looked straight down into the dragons' eyes. Suddenly the two dragons were calmed down as they both slowly lowered their bodies back onto the ground along with him. Krome remarkably understood that the twin dragons were the guardians of the secret plant. He kept his eye contact with the two dragons as he walked closer toward them. The dragons comprehended Krome's mind. He reached out both of his hands to touch the dragons' heads. The dragons turned out to be very friendly; they humbly lowered their heads to obey Krome. He then jumped over the water onto the rocky ground where the mysterious plants were growing. Krome recognized the appearance of the fruits which the giant eagle had brought for him to eat many days ago. He started to wonder why the dragons did not attack the bird. He looked at the eagle's eyes again; he now knew that they were both friends and the guardians of the plant.

"Why did you not tell your dragon friends that I am your friend too, Aerian? Looked like they wanted to eat me alive for a moment," Krome talked to the bird.

"I almost used this sword to chop off the heads of those two dragons or they could have eaten me alive . . . and you . . . you didn't even try to stop them." Krome said.

He continuously looked at the bird's eye and he understood what the bird wanted to explain to him about what had happened.

"Oh . . . I'm sorry. I knew you could not tell them because they were sleeping in the water. Yes, I got it, Aerian . . . that makes sense, my Angel Bird," Krome apologized.

Krome looked back at the Oradius plant; he did not see many fruits, only three left. He sat down to carefully observe the plant. He had never seen any species like this plant at all; it had the appearance close to a stone with rainbow colors. It had grown with seven large leaves about three feet from the top of the rock as its crystal roots had grown into the rock. He tried to pick one of the leaves but it was as firm as the strength of steel. Only the stems where it grew and produced the fruits were like the stems of normal trees. Krome analyzed the plant as he sensed its energy with his hands. Now he knew the plant had been living about the same age of the planet and not like other organic plants, Oradius had its own spiritual senses and cyberian energies. Every three thousand years this immortal plant had grown nine flowers which produced nine fruits. Each fruit had different molecular energy and when the nine fruits were combined together it would form into a single constant source of energy. Krome used his psychic power to connect and communicate with the plant's spiritual channel; he sensibly comprehended the entire process and the purpose of the immortal fruits.

"A person must eat all nine fruits to become completely immortal. The first step, a person must eat only six fruits, he or she will sleep for six days then a person will wake up. The second step, a person must wait until the next three days then he or she can eat the last three. If the nine fruits are consumed at once, the person will sleep forever and a body will turn into a stone." Krome repeated his insight acknowledgment.

Krome finally realized why the bird only brought him

six fruits. He could eat the last three in the following next three days.

"Thank God! I did not eat the last three fruits today," Krome spoke in his mind with relinquishment. "That could turn my body into a stone . . . very close to a stone man."

The two dragons jumped onto the rocky ground and moved close to Krome. They both looked at Krome, nodding their heads up and down then they jumped back into the water. He comprehended the dragons' minds; they wanted to go back into the water. Krome stood up and stretched his body, looking for a spot to sit down. He moved to the other side of the plant and sat down next to it. He closed his eyes and started to meditate again as he waited until the next three days.

"I wanted to warn you about the two golden green dragons and the processes of eating the immortal fruits but you have left me too soon, Krome," Aquarus again appeared in Krome's vision and explained to him.

"Now I am very glad that you are safe and have found out about the secret of this magical plant. One more thing that I would like to warn you is very, very important; you must protect this secret plant not to have it destroyed or your immortality will turn back to cyberian and the planet will be destroyed too. It is very hard for cyberians to reach the top of this mountain, at the bottom it is surrounded by a very deep, strong stream of the river and many dragons are living down there as the guardians. As you can see from the top of this mountain, the big river is flowing strong from the north then it is divided into two and each is flowing around the mountain. One separates the other mountains and your valley from it on the north side; the other one separates the other mountains on the south side. Then these two rivers meet again near the west side flowing into the ocean. Even the God of Darkness could not see this place because this place is also protected by the God of the Enlightenment," Aquarus explained.

"Your village was protected by the Holy Spirit because you are God's destiny and your people are good people. Your people have never wanted to find this plant; they only wanted to escape from the danger and the bad people. Otherwise, they could not live in that valley down there. I had fought in many battles, most for fairness and honesty. Even myself, I had never realized the whole truth of the secret plant and the purpose of the eternal life; not until I died. I've learned many things; God has shown me all the purposes of life. Now my soul has become a Holy Spirit, I'm happy to guard this place and to stay up here. No temptation, no killing, no war, no suffering, in front of me it is only one purpose, that is, the enlightenment. I'm happy to become immortal on this planet. Thus, I'm able to cross the universe in no time; talking about time, time is not matter in my world. I didn't regret not eating the fruits if I succeed to get to the fruits. I would eat them all at once and I definitely would turn into stone. But you . . . you are different," Aquarus continued.

"What do you mean? I mean that . . . I'm different," Krome asked.

"You . . . you are not who you think you are; you are the purpose of God, your destiny is to protect the enlightenment from the darkness, to lead good people against the evil in cyberian or any animal forms," Aquarus answered.

"Will I live forever like this? I mean in my cyberian body," Krome curiously asked.

"No, you'll probably live for nine hundred thousands

of years from now and this is about three hundred twenty-eight and a half million years in the cyberian world. At the end of nine hundred thousand years, you'll transform into the Holy Spirit or the Evil Spirit, depending on what you would do in this nine hundred thousand years. If you will do all good things, you will stay in the enlightenment forever. Or if you decide to do all the bad things then you will be stuck in darkness forever," Aquarus explained.

Krome took a deep breath as he tried to remember all Aquarus's explanations.

"I see. I still have so many obligations and works to be done on this planet. And it will be very long, long time for me to spend on this planet," Krome said with his deep breath.

"Why, Krome? Are you bored already? This is just your beginning," Aquarus said.

"No . . . No, I am happy but nine hundred thousands of years, I think a little bit too long for me. Don't you think so Aquarus?" Krome told Aquarus.

"Three hundred twenty-eight and a half million years in cyberian life, oh God I forget that one day up here it is one year down there in the cyberian world," Krome complained.

"Well Krome don't feel too bad, by the time you realize maybe it is three hundred twenty-eight million and four hundred ninety-nine thousand years already then maybe you will wish it could have been longer than this." Aquarus tried to encourage Krome.

"I'm your guidance. If you need help, I'll assist you but only with the good purpose. Besides, I think you will be alright on your own. And one last thing I need to remind you again, one day up here is one year in the cyberian world. Did you see your body has grown? You're now eighteen years old and in the next three days you must eat the last three fruits to turn your body into complete immortality," Aquarus explained.

Three days had passed by as fast as Krome silently sat in his quiet meditation and interestingly communicated with Aquarus. He opened his eyes and turned around to pick up the last three fruits. Krome fully turned into immortal form after he ate the rest of the fruits. Now he felt strange inside his body, he did not even feel his own heart beat. Inside his body everything was so calm, so peaceful; he did not even feel his body weight. He looked at the big rock, thinking that he could lift it; suddenly the rock was floating into the air. He thought he could fly to the top of the mangrove tree then his body was swiftly moved to the top of the tree. Krome knew that he had possessed the power close to God; he was able to use the unseen forces surrounding him to control the objects. Then the two golden dragons again jumped out the pond attacking Krome constantly; they threw the big flame of fire at him. Krome drew and held his sword with both hands straight up next to his chest as he sat spinning his body into the air in the middle of the flame. He looked at the dragons' eyes trying to tell them to stop but they did not respond. Krome felt he did not want to destroy the two dragons. He used the unseen force to hold the dragons down; he could feel their mighty strength resisting his power. He thought he could tie the two dragons' bodies together then gradually the bodies of the two dragons were bound together by a single rope. He slowly put them back onto the ground while his body was still floating in the air. They stayed still in one place as Krome moved closer. He looked at the dragons again now he knew the dragons had surrendered and it was the real test of his inner spiritual power. He untied the two dragons and he petted their heads gently. The dragons bowed their heads to respect Krome's mighty power and great wisdom.

Now Krome turned twenty-one; he looked truly attractive as the young, most handsome, muscular warrior; he resembled an angel's appearance. He closed his eyes and tried to communicate with Aquarus again.

"Congratulations, Krome, now you are immortal and you possess the power of God. You must use it wisely. I've seen the true wisdom and great force in you when you battled the two dragons. You controlled your mind and judged it very well to spare the lives of the two dragons. I know that you need to save your mother and your brother. Before you make a trip to Almar Kingdom, you must first go to Samatean Kingdom because you must save Princess Adelia from the evil sacrifice to the giant snake, named Serpenum. She will be eaten by this giant snake in the next seven days. Your family's situations will be safer than hers, again use your wisdom and force only with good intentions," Aquarus explained.

Krome turned around and walked toward the giant bird. He took a last look at the bird. He talked to the eagle as he petted its neck.

"Again, thank you, Aerian, for saving my life to become immortal. You are my true Guardian Angel. I'll see you again soon. I wish you could come along but this is the place where you belong. You must protect the secret plant with your two dragon friends . . . I'll be back . . . this is my home too," Krome said.

Krome waved goodbyes and turned around throwing himself into the air like a bird from the top of the Aquarium Mountain.

"I'll see you again, Aquarus, Aerian, my Guardian Angels and my two dragon friends. . . . I'll be back with all of you again," Krome said.

Krome threw his body down from the giant rock and flew down the mountain. He stopped by his village before he traveled to the Samatean Kingdom. He used his supernatural power to carve the stone into the funerary monument to bury all the bones, which belonged to his father, and his people who were killed in the battle by Valimus's armies. He looked at the place where he used to play with his brother and friends for the last time and paid the last tribute in front of the monument then he flew west toward the Samatean Kingdom to save Princess Adelia.

5

Protus Becomes an Almar Warrior

Back in Almar Kingdom, over nine years went by as Protus turned into his eighteenth birthday. Valimus treated Protus like his own son because he wanted to make Merida fall in love with him. He had become the most trusted man to King Hemiro after he safely returned from the Aquarium Mountain. Wizard Diron had released his evil spell from Princess Hollidia; she became well and the King was very happy with his work. Diron had increased his magic power stronger after the sacrifice of the life of the silver horn unicorn, he made to the God of Darkness with one of the suspicious boys who he had thought to be the holy child. Valimus ordered his best men to train Protus as he tried to impress Merida; he hoped one day he could win over her heart. Protus learned all the battle skills as his body had grown into the mighty muscular warrior. No one in the kingdom could ever defeat his strength or his fighting skills. Valimus pretended he was proud of Protus as Merida passed by and he wanted to show his compassion to her.

"Protus, you must learn these skills harder because you will be the future leader, the new general of my armies," Valimus said.

"Yes, Lord Valimus, I want to be the best and the

greatest champion in this whole kingdom . . . and thank you for your kindness, my lord," Protus answered.

Protus answered Valimus with his arrogant attitude as his life was spoiled by Valimus in the last nine years in Almar Kingdom.

"Merida, my dear lady, do you see what I've done for your beloved son? I have only good intentions. Please accept my heartedly humble proposal. My true love I ever have for you," Valimus said.

Valimus talked with Merida as he pulled her hands up close to his heart.

"You're always in my heart. I've risked my life just to bring you back here, just to see your beautiful face and spend the rest of my life with you," Valimus said.

"Let me go . . . I hope that one day Protus will cut your head for Optimus," Merida said.

She angrily pushed Valimus aside and walked away from him. He tried to stop her but at the same moment King Hemiro walked out from the hall a distance toward him.

"Lord Valimus how is our army doing these days? I would like some of your best men to guard my daughter, Princess Hollidia to visit the Almar's shore and pay respects to the Queen's tomb tomorrow," King Hemiro ordered.

"Your majesty, I'll assemble my men at once, your highness," Valimus said.

He answered the King then he turned to look at Protus. He apologized to the king.

"Your majesty, please forgive me, your highness," Valimus excused.

"Protus, I'll use you to accompany Princess Hollidia as one of my best men on the trip tomorrow. This opportunity will gain you a good experience," Valimus said.

"My lord, thank you for this great opportunity," Protus answered Valimus.

"Your majesty, I'll protect Princess Hollidia from all harm if anything happens to her. Her precious life is my life, my king," Protus assured the king.

Protus tried to ensure the safety of Princess Hollidia with King Hemiro. He could not remember his past at all, especially the death of his father at the Freewill because Wizard Diron drugged his mind. He did not even remember his brother. He became an aggressive person and turned into a barbarian, merciless warrior; he always took his opponent's soul. Killing to him was just like a game of battle. Valimus could not force or use his power over Merida because she was King Hemiro's cousin. He could only play a cold politic with her but inside he was burning. Valimus had asked Merida to marry him but she had refused his request each time. He put her in the palace and watched her like his own prisoner. He climbed up the stairs to one of the rooms on the top of the wizard castle where Diron presided.

"My dear Wizard Diron, how is your magic doing these days? Do you think your magic power can control Lady Merida's mind? I have a job for you; if you succeed, I'll reward you many gifts including Princess Hollidia," Valimus said.

Valimus asked Diron as he walked into the room and closed the door behind his back. Diron was very surprised when he heard the Princess Hollidia was among the gifts.

"Lord Valimus, are you joking with me? I'm afraid that King Hemiro will remove our heads," Diron replied with his timid smile.

"Hah, hah, hah, hah . . . remove our heads. . . . Hum; I am thinking that King Hemiro should be removed from his throne. He has been a king for too long," Valimus acted.

Valimus laughed to assure his conversation and bravely spoke to Diron. He continued as he moved to sit on one of the chairs next to the wizard stone table.

"My dear Wizard . . . My wizard of arc, can you read my mind? If not, I think your magic power will be useless. I've been planning to crown myself as the king for . . . for some time, don't you know that?" Valimus said.

Diron reassured himself with his big, ugly smile as he captured all of Valimus's conversation, then he used it to reclaim his creditability.

"Well, Lord Valimus, now you're telling me the whole truth, the truth that was on my mind for a long time. I've wanted to ask you this matter for many times in the past but I was afraid you would be upset and hold me as a traitor against the king," Diron said.

He humbly moved close to tap Valimus's left shoulder as he tried to encourage and show respect to Valimus.

"Lord Valimus, I know you have the power to do this. You have the control of the whole armies and many of your strong men; they all listen to you, they will do whatever you say. Heh, heh, heh . . . if I am not wrong, you want to conquer Lady Merida's heart. But to do so, you must . . . you must remove the king first," Diron said.

Valimus pointed his finger into the air as he saw Diron's reaction and expression.

"Now you've got my point. You're very clever, my Wizard. After all you are seeing all the action in this kingdom. I'm glad that you're on my side, Wizard Diron. Do you know? The only person I trust is you . . . you're my wizard of arc," Valimus said.

"You will be a great king, I mean better than King Hemiro. I've always been working with you since the

41

past, Lord Valimus. There will be nothing can ever stop me . . . stop me from serving you, my King." Diron excitedly expressed himself to Valimus.

Valimus proudly stood up and patted his hand on Diron's shoulder as he was ready to leave. He tapped Diron's shoulder to remind him of his request.

"Wizard Diron, you are my right hand man . . . better than my armies. If we succeed, I'll let you rule this kingdom by my side. We have to be careful because some leaders are still very loyal to King Hemiro. First we have to eliminate all these people. I'll discuss with you more about this, but for now you have to turn Merida's mind to fall in love with me. I hope you will not let me down . . . my dear Wizard," Valimus said.

After Valimus had left, Diron looked around to gather all his witchcraft materials to prepare for his evil spell to control Merida's mind. He softly whispered to himself with his hands a little bit shaky as he suddenly hungered for Princess Hollidia's sweet love.

"Oh my precious Princess Hollidia, my beloved angel. I want to taste your heavenly body. . . . She is very beautiful . . . oh, hoh, hoh," Diron whispered.

Diron was a virgin man since the time he had become a wizard. He had never tasted a woman in his entire life. The beauty of Princess Hollidia could blind his soul; he would die for her appearance. She just turned seventeen and all young men in her kingdom could not resist her royal character and charm. She rarely came out of the castle or walked around the palace. Everywhere she went there were always royal mates and guards to accompany and protect her. Diron had never dreamt or thought about Princess Hollidia before he had the conversation with Valimus. His mind now filled with strong temptation, contaminated with sexual desire; he could be asked to do anything for this reward. Valimus and his magical power. Diron knew if he touched the women all his magical powers would fade away. In the return, he could have Princess Hollidia and gained his royal power in the kingdom as Valimus agreed and promised to share his power with him.

"I would like each of you to watch out for all dangers and to safeguard the Princess. Anyone who does not obey my order will be executed. Understood?" Protus said.

"Yes! My lord." Soldiers answered altogether.

The sound of the royal horn acknowledged the arrival of the royal family in front of the castle as King Hemiro accompanied his daughter, Princess Hollidia, along with Meridia, other royal leaders and Valimus toward the front court. Protus stood very straight with his left hand holding the sword handle next to his waist.

"Your majesty, Lord Valimus, our armies are ready, my king . . . my lord," Protus said.

"Well, Lord Valimus, I am very comfortable that Protus goes along to protect my beloved daughter. He is the strongest man in our kingdom," King Hemiro said.

The king turned to Valimus and showed his concern for the safety of his daughter.

"I'm more worried than ever because now the Princess has grown into a beautiful young lady. More men have strong desires toward her. But with you and Protus, I feel completely confident and I will be in peace of mind at my castle," King Hemiro said.

Valimus quickly replied to the King, as he felt a little bit uncomfortable with the king's conversation. He knew himself, the one who tried to bring chaos to this kingdom because of his strong desire for the absolute powers and Merida's heart.

"Your majesty, Princess will be safe and have a won-

43

derful time. She will be back here very safe in the next seven days, my king," Valimus reassured the king.

Protus humbly lowered his head and helped to hold Princess Hollidia's hand as she stepped up on into the royal wagon.

"Be careful with your steps . . . your highness," Protus said.

She turned around to take a look at Protus and gave him a smile. Protus got lost for a moment then he again bowed his head to obey the Princess as he let go of her hand into the wagon. He turned around to bow to King Hemiro, Valimus, and Merida before he got up on the back of his horse. Protus and Valimus rode on the horses ahead of the Princess's wagon and they traveled west toward the ocean shore.

"Protus, what do you think about Princess Hollidia? I've not really recognized that she has grown into a very pretty lady after all these years," Valimus said.

Valimus wanted to test Protus's mind and to see his feeling toward the princess as he continued to steer the conversation about Princess Hollidia.

"Her age and yours are almost the same age; it is only one year apart. Besides you are the King's long distant nephew . . . you too have grown to be a handsome man," Valimus said.

"Lord Valimus, I don't really understand. What do you mean, my lord?" Protus asked.

"Let me tell you, Protus, your mother, Merida is King Hemiro's cousin and you're the King's distant nephew. I don't blame you because your parents have never told you about this but I . . . I like you as my own son," Valimus explained.

"Lord Valimus, I know that you always look after me.

I wish my mother could see your sympathy and kindness, my lord," Protus gratefully answered.

"Hah, hah, hah . . . I'm happy that you're able to see and feel this way. I hope someday she will change her mind. Do you agree with her? Let's say, if one day she decides to marry me." Valimus laughed and continued his conversation.

"My lord, I respect you like my own father. If this could happen, I'll be happy for both of you and stand against any who want to hurt my parents. And for Princess Hollidia, I believe I'll surrender to her beauty . . . my lord," Protus said.

Valimus felt so relieved after he heard Protus's words. He knew Protus had the hearty feeling for Princess Hollidia. He thought this would easily control Protus so as to control Diron. He knew man's weakness was the beauty of woman.

The sun almost down, Princess Hollidia and her armies decided to camp out near the small lake by the hillsides for the night. She was impressed with countryside views as she stood and looked a distance upon the green hill, crystal clear lake, and the vast mountain ranges at the background.

"This is so beautiful. Look at the sun, Protus; I've not seen this for a long time and look at those birds and those wild flowers," Princess Hollidia said.

Princess Hollidia met Protus a few times since he returned to Almar. She had never seen how he treated other men or his opponent. Each time she met him he looked different. Now Protus had grown into a handsome man with a strong, muscular body. She was amazed by his charm too.

"Princess Hollidia, how is your ride, your highness?

This will be our long ride and I think you probably are tired, your highness," Protus said softly.

She gave him a big lovely smile and flirtatiously answered as she was attracted to his charming appearance.

"It is a bit rough but as long as Protus rides by my side I'll be happy," the Princess said.

Suddenly two strange men rode horses from a distance and they passed the dirt road where a few of Valimus's soldiers posted nearby. The soldiers talked with those two strangers for a while then they wanted to arrest them. The strange men resisted and jumped back on their horses and tried to escape. Protus saw this from a distance then he jumped on his horseback and rode faster to chase them. As he caught up closer behind them, he took out his bow and arrow. He aimed at the horse's neck; one by one, he brought both horses down. The soldiers finally arrested and brought the men back to show Valimus.

"Protus you know what to do," Valimus told Protus.

Protus angrily questioned the two men why they wanted to run away as he beat and kicked them. They did not answer and he drew his sword to threaten them.

"For the last time, why did you two run away when my soldiers tried to stop you? Do you want to assassinate the Princess. Maybe you are spies," Protus interrogated the men.

"No please, we are just the traders from Amoza Kingdom. Please don't kill us, we never planned to hurt the princess or anyone," the men answered.

The two men answered with their hands shaking as they knew they would be dead in a few moments, Protus ordered his soldiers to give their swords back to them.

"You are from Amoza. If you want to walk away with

46

your lives, you two must defeat me first. Here is your sword . . . get up and fight with me," Protus said.

The two men clearly understood the rule of the engagement of Almar Kingdom so they grabbed their swords ready to fight with Protus. Protus thought this would be a good show for Princess Hollidia; two fought against one. The men were good swordsmen as they both fought fiercely with Protus. The soldiers wanted to help but Protus ordered them to stay out. He was a champion swordsman in Almar kingdom, besides this was the show for Princess Hollidia. He spun his body into the air with a heavy long sword toward the two men. As his feet touched the ground, he cut the head of one man. Then he flipped his body up into the air again as the other man ran swinging the sword toward him. Protus lifted his body over the man; he slashed the sword at the man's neck. The man fell down instantly when Protus landed behind him. Protus felt so proud as he turned to look at the Princess. Princess Hollidia felt very disappointed; she thought the killing could be avoided because this was the trip to pay a tribute and respect for her mother's soul. This could have been a peaceful trip. She spoke to Protus with her regret as she did not want to see this incidence.

"What is happening? Why does there have to be killing?" the Princess said.

Protus arrogantly answered Princess Hollidia as he tried to convince the princess that the two men were the real assassins from Amoza Kingdom. He explained if they were good people, they would not try to run away from him in the first place.

"Princess, they are the spies and want to hurt you, your highness. Their combat skills are very dangerous as you could see that they fought harder and they even to want to kill me . . . don't you see that your highness?" Protus convinced the princess to believe him.

She had seen the whole incident; she did not feel the same way, the two men were not a threat to her. Probably they were the real traders; she thought in her mind. The great glamorous feelings which she just had for Protus this whole day were slowly fading away after she saw how rude and merciless he was toward the men. Princess Hollidia was also an intellectual young lady too as she tried to hide her certain feeling from Protus.

"Thank you for the protection, Protus. You are willing to risk your life for me. I truly appreciate that. . . . I think you should take a rest now," Princess Hollidia said.

He replied and walked closer to her; he bowed at the princess with a respectful attitude.

"Your highness, this is my duty to protect you from all dangers. Your safety is my concern and your precious life is my life," Protus said.

Protus thought he had really impressed Princess Hollidia. He knew she truly appreciated his exertion.

"Forgive me; I need to rest because I'm tired from the long ride. I will see you tomorrow," the Princess said.

She spoke with a lovely smile as she went inside her tent. Protus's heart was filled with delightful romantic dreams; he stood still watching all her moves. Protus wanted to reassure Princess Hollidia's mind that his effort was serious. Then he decided to walk to the front of Valimus's tent, spoke louder so the princess could hear him.

"My lord, I think the two men were secret agents from Amoza kingdom because their sword skills were better than the average swordsmen," Protus said.

Valimus opened his tent and stepped out to talk to

Protus. He wanted Protus to be careful for the safety not just for Princess Hollidia but as well as for himself.

"I agree with your thought. Protus, you must order our soldiers to divide into small groups and post out around the camp. Tell them to take high precaution tonight there might be more of them out here," Valimus said.

"Yes my lord, I will act at once," Protus replied with his attention.

He jumped on his horse's back, rode toward the soldiers, and ordered them to spread out into a small group to surround the camping ground.

"I want three men in each group, you must take turns for your rest and you must be aware tonight, there may be more of them out here. You must watch out, understood? I want all of you to spread out posting around not too far from Princess Hollidia's tent and I want more men along the side of that road!"

Protus rode the horse back to his tent and sat on the rock looking toward Princess Hollidia's tent with his romantic imagination.

"Princess Hollidia is very beautiful and kind. She didn't even want me to kill the two men; the way she has questioned me. I've met her a few times but this is the first time that she has talked to me. At least she appreciates my action," Protus said.

He remembered the moment he held her hand this morning, her lovely smile outside the tent. He leaned his body against the rock trying to remember further into his past. Then suddenly his head grew dizzy and he was so agitated mentally as the evil spell and drug of Diron became less effective against his memories. He seemed to be helplessly fighting back with this commotion. Valimus rapidly appeared in front of him as he remembered

49

Diron's advice that this sign would happen when Protus started to remember his past.

"What is it wrong with you, Protus? Did you get hurt from the fight?" Valimus said.

He pretended with his awareness as he knew the effect of the drug inside Protus became weaker and Protus's memories started to come back slowly.

"Here is some medication would make you feel better. I think you should take a rest. This drug will calm down your mind," Valimus said and gave the drugs to Protus.

The night was quiet and inside Princess Hollidia's tent two royal mate women slept next to the Princess. Princess Hollidia could not sleep at all then she had heard some disturbing noises. She carefully stood up and watched Protus from inside of her tent; she began to wonder why Protus acted strangely that way. She thought in her mind maybe he got hurt from the fight or he had a chronic illness.

"Could not be . . . impossible, I've just saw him a moment ago; he was feeling very fine. His body doesn't have any injuries . . . he is completely healthy," Princess Hollidia thought.

She decided to come out and ask him but she changed her mind when she saw Valimus show up. She wondered why Valimus gave the drug to Protus.

"Why did Lord Valimus give this kind of drug to Protus? This is the drug to help people forget their pasts and fears . . . why?" Princess thought.

She remembered she took these pills before. Especially the days she was very ill, she had many bad dreams, seeing devils haunting her. She recalled Diron told her father that this drug helped to calm down her mind and forget the fears. She thought maybe Protus had some bad memories or fears of his past. It was late for bedtime, then Princess Hollidia decided to go back to sleep. She did not want to disturb Protus, besides, it would not be appropriate to go to his tent in the late night like this.

"Good morning Protus, how do you feel? Are you sick?" Princess Hollidia asked. Princess Hollidia curiously questioned Protus as he opened his tent and stepped outside.

"Good morning your highness, I am feeling fine. How was your sleep last night? You are up so early . . . your highness," Protus humbly said.

"Oh, I slept well last night that is why I woke up early this morning," the Princess answered.

"Protus, you seem to look fine with your health . . . don't you?" Princess said.

Princess Hollidia talked with her lovely smile; she pretended she did not know any thing about last night. But Protus thought Princess Hollidia must know what had happened to him last night the way she questioned him.

"The way she had asked me, she must have seen what happened to me last night. I think she would come out to ask me if she knew something was wrong with me. Well, she probably was in her sleep already," Protus thought and had a doubt on his mind.

Valimus spoke to Princess Hollidia as he walked out of his tent.

"Good morning Princess, looks like you are ready to go . . . your highness," Valimus said.

"Good morning Lord Valimus, well . . . I want to get there soon. I am very anxious to see my mother's tombstone," she replied.

"Protus, how do you feel? Is your head feeling better?" Valimus asked.

"Good morning Lord Valimus, I feel much better already, my lord," Protus said.

"You should order the soldiers to get ready. I think we should move out soon so today we will arrive there early," Valimus told Protus.

"I will inform the soldiers to move out at once . . . my lord," Protus said.

He got up on the horse's back and rode toward the soldiers.

"Well your highness, we are not far from the Queen's tomb. We should be there in the next few hours, your highness," Valimus informed Princess Hollidia.

Princess Hollidia looked out through her royal wagon's window as the sun was almost over the hill. She really enjoyed the ride and the views of the hills and the forest along the river bank. Protus and Valimus ordered the soldiers to move faster toward the Almar shore. Protus kept seeing Princess Hollidia's smile and his mind, as he was quiet and busy thinking about her on his horse's back next to Valimus.

"What is it on your mind, Protus? You look like you have thinking about something. Is it your headache again? I . . . I start to worry about you," Valimus said.

Protus restored his confidence from his romantic imagination with Princess Hollidia as he answered with his true feeling to Valimus.

"I am sorry Lord Valimus, do not worry about me, my lord. I am just thinking about Princess Hollidia. She is very beautiful and caring. She asked me this morning as if she knew what had happened to me last night, my lord," Protus said.

Valimus felt much better and he started to talk more about Princess Hollidia again.

"Well Protus, Princess Hollidia is kind and wise. I

have known her since her childhood. She rarely speaks to anyone but with you . . . you are maybe always on her mind as I could see in her. I think she likes you," Valimus said.

Protus appreciated Valimus's comment and thanked him for the medicines that he gave to him last night.

"Lord Valimus, thank you for last night. The medicine was really helpful. I think I could never repay you for your kindness and care that you always have for me. I would risk my life to protect you, my lord," Protus said.

Valimus reached out his hand to tap on Protus's shoulder as he had tried to show his appreciation and kindness.

"I am really proud to have someone like you by my side," Valimus said.

They finally arrived at the Almar shore and Princess Hollidia began the ceremony at the Queen's tombstone. She brought a lot of beautiful flowers to decorate on her mother's tomb; she kneeled down in front of the tomb with her silent prayers for a few moments.

"I come here every year to pay respect to my mother's soul. She was sick, then she passed away when I was five years old. She died on this shore in my arms as Wizard Diron stood watching us. Wizard Diron explained to me that he had prayed for my mother to become better but God was upset and took her soul away," Princess told Protus.

"I'm sorry to hear this sorrow, your highness . . . you must be missing her very much when she passed away at your young age, your highness," Protus said.

6

Diron's Loving Spell

In the wizard castle Diron put everything together and began to perform his magic spell on Merida's soul. He made two cyberian shapes from the clay, one man and one woman. The woman clay doll represented Merida and the man clay doll represented Valimus. He had placed Merida's clay doll on the stone tablet next to the jar which was filled with his black magic ingredients such as the beeswax, wild flowers and other plants, called the liquid of temptation, particularly for sexual urgency. He sat down with his eyes close and repeated the words in the wizard language to capture her soul and to arouse her heart to be in the mode of sexual desire. He warmed up the jar over the candle flame to melt the wax then he took a small brush and dipped it into the liquid of the wax. He then began to paint the wax on the forehead, on the chest, and on the belly button of the female clay doll as he repeated magic words. Now he placed both hands over the clay doll's body and he used his wizard power to spin it around seven times.

"This process is done. It will turn you on, Merida. You will run to Lord Valimus with your hungry eyes when I finish the other parts. You will beg him for his love. Your mind will fill with sexual desire, my dear lady . . . heh, heh, heh," Diron said.

Then he put Valimus's doll next to Merida's doll and began the second part of the spelling process. In the last part, Diron put the two dolls facing each other and tied them together with red strings made from cotton. The evil wizard laughed with positive results.

"Hah, hah, hah, hah, hah ... with these binding strings, Merida, you will fall for Lord Valimus until the time you die. You now belong to him," Diron whispered.

Merida stood inside her room looking through the window, thinking about Krome and Optimus; her tears were flowing down from her eyes. Her heart was full with sorrow. She felt even more agonizing to see Protus seem to lose his mind. She often thought to commit suicide, as she wanted to leave those painful memories behind. But the pureness of her belief in the God of the Enlightenment was deep inside her heart; therefore, she had a strong belief it would be very sinful and against God's will to take her own life away. Then mysteriously she felt so weak and short of breath; she decided to lie down on the bed. She felt very strange inside her body. She sensed her body temperature getting warmer and warmer than usual. She began to remember her first night with Optimus as she closed her eyes and recalled her first time of sexual fantasy. She embraced her body with the caress and she touched her lip as she was in her highest state of sensation. Suddenly she saw Valimus appear beside her bed and he slowly started to kiss her and caress her body. With this indefinite bodily feeling, she could not resist a man who tried to fulfill her fantasy. She touched his body gently and pulled him close to her chest. She softly began to murmur her excited voice next to his ear. She completely opened her heart to him and she could not even remember the hatred that she felt toward him.

Now Krome had reached the territory of Samatean

Kingdom and he looked for a place to rest and meditate. He wanted to see how his mother and his brother were doing as he closed his eyes and tried to connect his spiritual power with them. He saw his mother motion in her room, as she was so tempted with sexual desire. He investigated further in his vision and saw Diron had performed his evil magic and put the spell on her soul. Krome looked around inside Diron's room to find the evil witchcraft. He found the clay dolls, which represented the bodies of Merida and Valimus. He concentrated his inner spiritual power to turn the two dolls around so they were back to back in the binding spell. This was the only way he could save his mother from Diron's evil spell. Diron had no clue what would happen next. Krome even reversed the spell to protect his mother then he put the shield of the enlightenment around her soul. Her soul could not be touched by the force of darkness. When the dolls were back to back in the red binding strings, Merida would hate Valimus more. Krome also saw what had happened to Protus. He knew if he reversed the spell for his brother; he would be killed by Valimus. He decided to wait until the time he returned to Almar Kingdom.

Merida slowly awakened from her half sleep and was so ashamed of herself. She even hated Valimus ten times more than she used to. She thought maybe Valimus had used the black magic to put the spell on her. She started to pray to the God of the Enlightenment to protect her from all harms and the darkness. As she closed her eyes and kneeled down in her prayer next to her bed she was connected to Krome's inner spiritual power.

"Mother, you must be strong. I will rescue you from all these dangers and darkness. You will have the good life like you used to have again but now you must act closer to Valimus and you must pretend that you have fallen in love with him. He has used the black magic to charm your soul. This way, you could blind his mind and you will be safe until I return to Almar," Krome communicated with Merida's mind.

She heard her son's voice inside her head very clear. She thought probably Krome's soul still followed her. She began to pray for him; therefore, his soul could rest in peace by the side of the God of the Enlightenment.

"Krome, may your soul rest in peace by God's side. Please God, guide my husband and my son to find the enlightenment. Krome, I had always prayed for you and your father. Perhaps we will be reunited together again in the enlightenment," Merida said in her prayer.

She opened her eyes with doubt, as she felt so real with this daydream. She then stood up to look down from her window; she saw Protus and Princess Hollidia had returned from their trip. She felt so happy to see her son and the Princess safely returned. She hurriedly went down to meet and to greet them for their return.

"I'm very happy to see both of you had a safe trip. Princess Hollidia, you must be tired with this long journey, your highness," Merida said.

"Lady Merida, thank you for your thought. I had a great time on this trip because Protus is such a good warrior," Princess Hollidia said.

"Protus, my beloved son, I am concerned with your sickness," Merida said.

"Thank you, mother, for your concern. Lord Valimus has been so kind to us, he always takes good care of me," Protus told his mother.

Protus spoke with his gratitude as he turned to look at Valimus on the back of his horse.

"Lord Valimus, thank you for your generosity. Please

forgive me for my rudeness and bad behavior toward you in the past, my lord," Merida said.

Valimus jumped off from the horse with a great smile and surprise as he assumed that Diron's loving spell was really working with Merida. He reassured himself with a great characteristic of a gentleman and politely spoke to her.

"Oh Lady Merida, it is not such a hard feeling at all. I am very glad that we are getting along at last. At least you are able to see my kindness and my heart always opens the door for you. We should put the past behind us and start the new lives together. I would always want to spend the rest of my life with you," Valimus said with a great smile.

Merida pretended she would love to live by his side as she gave him a positive consideration along with her flirtingly lovely smile.

"Lord Valimus, please give me some time to think it over. I wanted to discuss this with my son, Protus and King Hemiro first," Merida said.

Valimus walked close to her, lifted her right hand up and kissed her fingers as he looked directly into her eyes.

"I will not force you to do this but I will be uneasy waiting for your positive answer, my beautiful Lady," Valimus said.

Valimus expressed his feeling with Merida; he anxiously waited to make it out with her. Merida showed her pretended act with a bashful smile; she knew she had to make Valimus believe her behavior. She thought if Protus could not kill Valimus she would do it herself to revenge her husband and Krome.

"I will make you fall for my charm and I will kill you for Optimus and Krome. You will pay for what you have done to my family," Merida thought in her mind.

She whispered in her mind as she looked at Valimus's eyes with a receptive state of mind, acting like she surrendered her heart and her soul to him. Valimus understood Diron's spell now was burning inside Merida's mind. He wanted to test her response as he further gave her a kiss on her cheek to see her reaction. She responded by squeezing his hand with her charming smile and she answered with her gratification.

"Thank you, Lord Valimus. Today I am happy to see all of you are safe from the trip. I have often prayed God to protect all of you, especially Princess Hollidia," Merida said.

Then King Hemiro walked out from the palace's hallway to greet his daughter and to thank Valimus and Protus for the safeguard of his daughter.

"Well done Lord Valimus, thank you for your loyalty to the King and thank you, Protus, for your dedication to protect Princess Hollidia. I'll order the palace to have a big feast tonight. Hah, hah, hah, hah, we will celebrate the memory of the Queen and the safe return of my princess." He spoke to Valimus and Protus.

"Your majesty, thank you for your recognition and generosity. This will be an exciting night for our kingdom, and long live the king," Valimus said.

"Long live your majesty, thank you for your pleasurable satisfaction and kindness to my services. I am proud to serve your highness and your kingdom," Protus said.

Protus also bowed to the king with his humble character as now he felt closer to Princess Hollidia than ever. Princess Hollidia turned to look at Protus for a moment and then she made a complimentary remark to her father.

"Protus is a good man, an honest warrior; he is always willing to risk his life to protect me. I saw his sacrifice during my trip. I truly appreciate his royal duty and honesty. I am also grateful to Lord Valimus who has made this trip a safe trip for me," Princess said. Protus felt like a champion in the ring of battle when he heard the princess's comment and he turned to bow to the princess to show his appreciation to her.

"Your highness, thank you for your courtesy and wisdom. I will stand to defend this kingdom from any dangers," Protus said.

Valimus felt like a king himself; he thought this would be a good night to celebrate his accomplishment over Merida's heart. He again kissed Merida's cheek as he was ready to leave to his room.

"I will see you tonight at the royal feast, dear Lady Merida," Valimus said.

"Your majesty, I will inform all the generals in the kingdom at once about the royal feast tonight," Valimus said.

In his mind, Valimus planned to kill all the leaders who were loyal to the king. He kept thinking how he was going to do this without getting caught before he killed the king. He knew he must plan it carefully. He saw Diron's wizard ability would be very useful as he doubtlessly realized that Diron's loving spell was powerful. He knew Merida's mind now was poisoned by Diron's magic spell and she became his doll.

"The night like this would be the perfect time to execute someone; one of these days this kingdom will be mine . . . watch out my king," Valimus thought on his mind.

He was thinking in his mind while he walked back and forth inside his room. Suddenly the soldier knocked on Valimus's door.

"Who is that?" Valimus asked.

"Lord Valimus, this is general Valkon, I am sorry to

disturb you but the king would like to have words with you, my lord," Valkon informed with his firm voice.

For a moment Valimus was really nervous; he thought maybe the king had found out about his secret conspiracy. He thought maybe Diron could have been betrayed him as he recognized not seeing Diron among those people who came to greet the princess.

"General Valkon, please could you wait for a moment? I need to dress up and get myself ready first," Valimus said.

Valimus asked Valkon to wait and he put back his army uniform and his sword. He knew this was usual for the Wizard; Diron rarely came out from his castle unless something was very important.

"If the king knows my plan, maybe he will have me arrested already. Or he might send more soldiers to my room, not just one general, or the king has already set up the plan to capture me, " Valimus guessed in his mind.

Valimus opened the door slowly as he still was not so sure why and what reason that the king wanted to see him again so soon. He tried to stay calm as he walked toward the king's guest room. Valkon pushed the door open and said to the king.

"Your majesty, Lord Valimus is here . . . your highness," Valkon addressed the king.

"Yes, please let him in . . . General," the king said.

Valimus walked in and bowed to the king as he tried to maintain his calmness and was ready to have conversation with the king.

"Your majesty, I have understood your highness would like to have words with me . . . my king," Valimus said to the king.

"Yes! Lord Valimus, my daughter explained to me that Lady Merida finally is getting along with you. This is a good opportunity for you to marry the royal family since she has changed her mind after all these years. I know she has hated you in the past because of Optimus. However Optimus had broken the law of my kingdom, he had lured my cousin and ran away without letting me or anyone know; thus, he deserved to die under your sword. I know you have been honest to me and my family. You have served me and my kingdom for quite a long time and this will bring us closer as a strong royal family. What do you think, Lord Valimus?" King Hemiro explained to Valimus.

Valimus answered the king with his gratitude as he felt completely released from all the suspicious opinions he had on his mind a moment ago.

"Your majesty, I truly appreciate your greatest wisdom and kindness your majesty had toward our citizens and myself. I have always loved Lady Merida but with your blessing, I will serve your majesty and your kingdom until the end of my time and long live the king, my king," Valimus said to the king.

Valimus acted so humble to King Hemiro and it was totally opposite inside his head for what he had planned to do with the king.

"Your majesty, do you have anything else on your mind beside this? Forgive me, your majesty for asking this question," Valimus asked the king.

"Hah, hah, hah, hah . . . I have no other words for now. I hope we will have a peaceful and a great feast tonight. Thank you Lord Valimus for your consideration and acceptance. You can leave now," The king laughed and said.

Valimus again kneeled down to bow to the king before he walked out of the king's guest room. He reconsidered he would go along with the king's plan to get married to Merida first. He knew his power in the kingdom would be greater, then he would easily accomplish his secret conspiracy to kill the king and take over the kingdom.

Valimus still did not believe himself and he decided he must see Diron as he hurriedly walked to the wizard's castle. He looked around before he knocked on the door.

"Wizard Diron, please open the door for me. I am Lord Valimus," Valimus said.

Diron quickly opened and looked outside his door to make sure no one was following Valimus. He then closed the door behind him and greeted Valimus.

"Oh Lord Valimus, you are back already. Congratulation, your request is done and no one could ever resist this binding spell of love. Her heart now is wide open for you, my future king," Diron said.

Valimus sat down with his comfortable mind after he heard Diron's words. He laughed to compose his feeling before he started his discussion with Diron.

"Hah, Hah, Hah, hah," Valimus laughed.

"Thank you so much, my precious Wizard. Our plan is working well. Merida totally changed her attitude toward me; she even let me kiss her. It is very amazing; your magic spell is burning inside of her right now. We must be careful every action we do and every word we have to say in this kingdom; otherwise, your head and mine will be cut off. Do you understand me, Wizard Diron? I remind you of this matter just for your own safety and my reputation," Valimus said.

Diron wondered what was on Valimus's mind. Maybe it was just a strong precaution he must take to protect both of them or maybe Valimus did not trust him.

"Yes! Lord Valimus, these are our lives, I have understood very clear and how can I leak it out to the other people. You seemed not to trust me at all. Do you?" Diron said.

"No, no, no . . . I trust you one hundred percent but this is just for the sake of our safety. I will decide to marry Merida soon because King Hemiro also has agreed with this idea. My power will be greater after I get married to her and my plan will be easier for us to achieve. Hah, hah, hah, hah. Tonight King Hemiro will have the big feast in the palace and I would like you to come along to join us and to have a good look at your future bride, Princess Hollidia. I will bring you your reward tomorrow, more gold . . . and . . . and of course Princess Hollidia; but you must be patient and wait until the king is disappeared first. Hah, hah, hah, hah, hah," Valimus said.

Diron felt like a prince himself, as he was constantly excited with his big ugly smile.

"Lord Valimus, I definitely wanted to go to see my beautiful Princess Hollidia. I have not seen her for quite a while, oh my beloved princess," Diron said.

He moved close to Valimus's shoulder and whispered at Valimus's ear; he laughed like a child with his dirty mood.

"Lord Valimus, maybe tonight is to be your best night to taste Merida's beauty. You must do it soon, don't let this opportunity pass by too easily. All you have to do is just lure her with many glasses of wine then she will be your . . . Heh, heh, heh, heh," Diron said.

In the King's palace the sounds of dance music were delightful as the groups of beautiful ladies performed traditional dances for the King and his guests in the ballroom. Valimus sat between Merida and Protus next to the king's table and he cheered up his wine glass to the king, Wizard Diron, Protus, and the other leaders.

"Long live the King, your majesty may your strength

64

and intelligence lead this kingdom with peace for a very long time. I wish your majesty have a healthy and long life. Long live your majesty ... long live the King," Valimus greeted the king.

"Long live the King, your majesty." Everyone replied after Valimus. Valimus poured the wine into another glass and gave it to Merida as he tried to cheer her up with the crowds. He put his hand around her shoulder and kissed her cheek.

"Please drink it my Lady. This one for your happiness and your future," Valimus said. She almost got up to leave but she calmed down her mind trying to stay cool and took the glass from Valimus. She pretended she enjoyed the feast as Valimus leaned to kiss her cheek again. She acted like she wanted him tonight but then she pushed him back with her tantalizing character to attract Valimus to fall into her trap.

"Please Lord Valimus, I am a little shy among these people; please could we wait until we are alone, tonight? Here is more drink for you, my lord," Merida said.

"Lord Valimus, I am happy for you that my mother has changed her mind. I think this will be good for all of us. Please accept my toast; this one is for your happiness and peaceful life . . . my lord," Protus said and toasted his wine glass to Valimus.

Protus continued drinking his wine and looked at Princess Hollidia as he felt that she should be sitting by his side. He often gave her a smile as his heart wanted to show how much he needed her. Valimus felt like a king himself enjoying the feast and he planed to lure Merida to fall into his sexual urgency tonight. She acted happily and continuously poured more wine into Valimus's glass; she tried to make him become drunk. She had planned to take his life tonight as he planned to have sex with her.

The feast was going on for many hours and now it was close to midnight. Merida began to feel a little bit drunk herself; she had never drunk more wine like this in her entire life. Valimus now moved like a drunken person; he looked around and saw most people were drunk and some of them even passed out. He stood up and grabbed Merida's body to come along with him to her room. She still had the full control over her body even though she felt a little bit drunk. She tried to show her strong sexual temptation to Valimus to blind his mind to really believe her. She acted as if she had lost her soul in the binding spell of Diron's magic. She looked around and saw even Protus had passed out too. The princess and the king had left early. She spoke to Valimus with her beautiful smile and sexually exciting commotion.

"Please let's go to my room, Lord Valimus. I really want you tonight," Merida said.

She got up with a girlish attitude and pulled Valimus's hand along with her. She closed the door of her room quietly and pushed Valimus onto her bed. She caressed his body to make him fall asleep but Valimus was a strong man, even with this amount of the wine he was still able to control his mind and strength. He pulled Merida's body close to his chest and tried to undress her while he kissed her neck. His body was a little trembling as he had waited for this moment for too long. He started to caress her body back as he slowly pulled her dress up along her silky leg up to her beautiful thigh.

"Oh my dear Lady Merida, you are so beautiful and you have not changed since the day I laid my eyes on you. We should have been doing this for a long . . . long time. Finally, you wildly open for me, my sweet Lady," Valimus excitedly whispered.

First Merida went along with his moves very well but

soon she knew Valimus had gone too far. She realized he was still strong and fully conscious. She then resisted him with her womanly strength; she could not even do it. She started to feel sorry for herself and started to think about Krome. She closed her eyes and started to pray for a miracle to happen to her. She felt completely helpless while she surrendered herself to his mighty strength. He turned over, put her body down on the bed and pulled both of her legs wide open as he was ready to conquer her heart and the beauty of her body. She kept trying to push him away but the influence of alcohol in her body seemed effectively to let her down. Merida just closed her eyes feeling definitely hopeless as Valimus held both of her arms down to the bed; he pulled her dress halfway down to her chest and kissed her lip then toward her chest slowly.

"What have I done to myself? Please help me, God. Please help me Krome, help me Optimus. God please help me." Merida silently prayed and called for help in her mind.

Gradually Valimus's strength began fading away as he was slowly getting weaker and weaker, then he fell into his sleep on her body. Merida rapidly opened her eyes and pushed him over to the other side of her bed and looked at him with her madness.

"Thank God, he finally passed out. This is will be your last night and this one is for both of you, Optimus and Krome . . . please forgive me God," Merida said.

She got up very quick to get the dagger under her bed and lifted it with her two hands higher into the air ready to stab him at his heart but for a moment she put down the knife slowly. She started to remember the King Hemiro's conversation with Valimus early today. Merida thought if she murdered Valimus the king would punish her and her son, Protus. For her life, it was not important but she was concerned about Protus's future and besides, it was against God's will to kill a person. Particularly a person who had no hatred toward her.

In Samatean Kingdom Krome saw all the actions in his meditation; he used his spiritual force to help his mother by emptying Valimus's strength from his body. He provoked her mind to remember the King's conversation with Valimus and showed her the purpose of the enlightenment. He sacked the angers inside her heart to spare Valimus's life and he thought she should leave it to Protus to revenge his father. Merida felt awful as she saw the dagger in her hand. She hid it back under her bed and kneeled down to begin a prayer to ask God for forgiveness.

"No, no . . . I can't do this. I just can't kill him. I'm sorry Optimus. I'm sorry Krome. Please forgive me, God. Please forgive me for the sin I'm about to commit," Merida said.

She cried with her sadness and closed her eyes and continued in her prayer as she tried to release her anger and hatred. Then again she had heard Krome's voice inside her head.

"Mother, please be strong and I will always be with you. When you need help, all you have to do is just to call my name. I will protect you from this darkness. I will be with you soon when I finish my assignment here. You must remember to call my name when you are in danger," Krome told his mother in her prayer.

She clearly heard Krome's voice inside her head. She stood up to look at Valimus then she went outside her room to ask the guards to take Valimus back to his room.

"Please guards, could you bring Lord Valimus back to

his room, I think he has too much drink for tonight. Please take a good care of him," she spoke to the guards.

She kept thinking about Krome's voice, which was so clear and real in her prayer.

"I believe Krome's soul protects me from all harm. Thank you, God, for saving me from this danger and sin." Merida said to herself.

She hoped one day Protus would be strong and remember what had happened to his father and his brother in Freewill Valley, then he would avenge them.

Diron left with the excitement when he saw Merida take Valimus into her room. He was proud of his wizard power. He was deep into his fantasy with Princess Hollidia's beauty. He hardly kept his evil eyes off her during the feast and sometimes he totally lost his mind. Back in his room, he started another spell on the princess; he began to assemble another clay doll shape to represent Princess Hollidia's body. He placed her body on the stone tablet next to a jar of the wax of temptation and put the melting wax onto a doll's body. He repeatedly whispered the witching words with his hands in the air over her body. He then looked into his magic glass ball to see the princess in her sleep. He used his black magic power to arouse the princess's sexual desire. Princess Hollidia slowly moved in her sleep with strong sexual agitation as she murmured softly and spread her arms on her silky bed. She felt like someone gently caressed her body. Diron was looking through the magic ball and his hands started to become shaky.

"Oh, my beautiful Queen, my precious Princess, you are an absolute angel. I will be your prince one of these days." Diron whispered.

He was as tempted as he saw the princess move her lovely legs and body with her unconscious sensation. He continued his spell faster and faster trying to put more heat into the princess's body so she would undress herself. Suddenly he stopped with his surprised move because the magic ball was broken into two pieces and the view was fading away.

"My God of Darkness, please forgive my temptation. I do not mean to touch her; I just want to see her body. Oh my magic ball, what has happened to you?" Diron regrettably said.

Diron did not realize that Krome channeled his power from a far distance to overwrite his wizard power and break his magic ball. Krome was smiling with his eyes closed; he knew this was so funny to see the evil action of the wicked wizard who was filled with an evil mind and temptation which he called love.

"Sorry Diron, the show is over. You are the force of darkness. One day we will collide and your dark power will surely fade away. Soon I will meet you face to face, you must be prepared against the power of the Enlightenment," Krome whispered in his mind.

Diron picked up his magic ball and wondered why it had broken into two. He thought maybe Princess Hollidia must possess with some kind of power which was stronger than his magic power. He tried harder with his wizard power to figure out what would be the possibility but he still could not understand the real cause.

7

Krome Rescues Princess Adelia

Six days had passed by fast as Krome readied to battle with the powerful giant serpent, called Serpenum. He sat on the rock behind the trees next to a great lake by the mountain side; he waited silently to see Princess Adelia. He heard the noises from far away like the sound of older woman crying in deep sorrow. He saw the group of the soldiers with the king, queen, and Princess Adelia travel in the panic appearances; the queen cried with her sorrows as she was about to lose her lovely daughter.

"My beloved Adelia, my dear princess, I will die by your side. I do not want you to sacrifice yourself alone to God Serpenum. I would rather die for you," the queen said.

"Please my dear Lady, my queen; you must understand God Serpenum's will. He will be very angry and he will destroy our kingdom. He only wants Princess Adelia alone and no one else can ever take her place. I am the King but I cannot even save my daughter's life. Oh God, what can I do?" The king said and begged the queen to leave.

Princess Adelia comforted her mother and asked her to leave the place. She knew the snake could come any time.

"Mother, please, you must go back to the palace. It is

almost time for God Serpenum to come up and take me. If you all are still here, you all will be killed. I happily sacrifice my body just to save all innocent people in our kingdom. Please go, mother, I beg you . . . you must go back . . . please go back, mother," Princess Adelia said to the Queen.

"Adelia, my beloved daughter . . . may God bless your soul . . . I want to die with you, my only child . . . oh God, please help her," the queen said in her tears.

The soldier brought Princess Adelia to the top of the big rock near the water of the great lake and they tied her hands with the rope and the other end of the rope was tied to the wooden post on the rock, preventing the princess from escape. The king had ordered the soldier to take the queen back to the palace. Princess stood hopelessly waiting to be eaten by the giant snake as Krome still hid quietly behind the trees not far from her to observe what would happen next.

The sun was almost up straight overhead and suddenly the dark clouds were blocking the light over the great lake and the mountain. The lightning struck through the thick dark clouds down into the water. Rapidly the water in the lake was moving with the huge waves; Krome sensed the giant snake slowly rose from the bottom of the lake. He quickly flew to the rock where Princess Adelia was tied down onto the post. She was very astonished to see Krome appear from nowhere and stand next to her.

"Who are you? You must leave this place at once, the God of the Snake is coming. He will kill you if he sees you here," Princess asked and demanded Krome to leave.

"My name is Krome. I'm your saver and I will defeat this giant snake today. I've traveled from a far away mountain. Princess Adelia, please give me your hands, I will cut you loose first," Krome calmly introduced himself.

She observed with doubt as she lifted both of her hands up toward Krome.

"How come you know my name? If you do not live in this kingdom, or you . . . you must be the warrior who my father has hired you to save me," Princess Adelia guessed.

"No, Princess, someone else has sent me here to save you, be quick your hands. Please be hurried, we don't have much time . . . the snake is coming," Krome continued.

He used his dagger to cut the rope around Princess Adelia's hands loose as the snake rose up to the surface of lake and moved toward the rock where they stood.

"Here, hold on to this dagger for me and hide behind this rock," Krome said.

Krome told the princess to hide behind the rock as he saw the big snake move toward him. He instantly floated into the air and flew toward the snake. Princess Adelia was very amazed to watch Krome and the snake without a blink of her eyes.

Krome flew up straight to the head of the snake; he looked at the snake eyes trying to communicate with the mind of the serpent. He knew the snake demanded him to leave if he wanted to live. The snake wanted just Princess Adelia and it would go back into the water.

"Serpenum, the God of the Snake, you must return to the bottom of the lake and spare Princess Adelia's life. You must leave the people in her kingdom with no harm and I will spare your . . . please leave at once!" Krome talked to the snake.

"Sheee, sheee, who are you dare to disturb my meal? Every one hundred years I have come up here just to swallow my bride so her soul will be with me forever. I have been living here for over nine thousand years in this lake and have swallowed many souls. Why do you dare to stop me today?" the snake talked back to Krome.

"Sheee, sheee, you probably do not want to live, then I will swallow you too, cyberian creature," the snake warned Krome.

Adelia was so amazed with the speaking ability of the snake and its enormous size; she had never seen a snake that was very big like this one.

"Talking snake, you are the force of darkness. You must leave the people in Samatean Kingdom with peace or your life will be ended today!" Krome demanded the snake.

Serpenum rapidly swung its head toward Krome and missed him. Krome raised both of his hands up into the air, absorbing the lightning bolt from the dark clouds above him as he stood in the middle of the air above the snake. He transformed the lightning into a huge light ball and fired it directly at the snake's head.

"Kaaboom . . . Boom!" the explosion blasted.

The blasting sound echoed over the great lake louder than the thunderbolt struck the earth. The snake suddenly fell down back into the water while Krome still floated in the air.

Krome looked down to the spot where the snake had fallen. Again Serpenum moved out of the water and flew straight and sprayed out poisonous venom toward him. He flew up faster and higher; he used his inner spiritual power to wrestle with the snake. The snake tumbled down on the ground as Krome threw it back down to earth. However, the snake kept coming back at him and the snake even used its inner spiritual force to throw the giant rock at him. Krome's mighty power was greater than the snake as it collided with the rock; it exploded into a zillion pieces, scattering all over the lake. The battle was going on for hours and Krome finally decided to use Aquarus's mighty sword to kill the snake. He flew back down toward the snake with both hands holding the sword, aiming straight down at its head as the snake flew up straight toward him. With an unseen force and Aquarus's mighty sword, Krome slashed the snake's body into two equal parts from the head to the tail after the two collided. The dark blood of the snake fell back into the lake; it caused the water to become red like the fruit punch in the big bow. Krome took the soul of the giant serpent and he helped to release ninety princesses' souls that were trapped in the body of the snake. The snake would extend its life every one hundred years after it swallowed each virgin princess alive. The snake body was floating on the water inside the great lake as Princess Adelia stood up and held her breath to watch Mighty Krome battle with the giant snake. He flew back down and landed next to her; he turned back to look at the dead snake as it started to decompose and then it turned into smoke.

"Are you alright Princess? This has taken longer than I thought. He was quite a snake of his own size and powerful too," Krome said without looking at Princess Adelia.

Princess Adelia was completely speechless as she looked at Krome without a blink in her eyes. She slowly walked around him and she kept looking at him closely from his head down to his toes with wondering.

"Amazing!" Princess Adelia said as she kept walking around him.

"Very amazing! Not a single scratch or a drop of blood . . . are you God?" Adelia asked.

"You must be the angel at least, if I'm not wrong," Princess Adelia continued.

She kneeled down and bowed to worship Krome as she still held on to his dagger.

"Thank you for saving my kingdom and my life, my Guardian Angel. I don't know how I can ever repay my life back to you," Princess Adelia said.

Krome lowered his body closer to Princess Adelia and asked for his dagger back.

"Please . . . can I have my dagger back, your highness?" Krome asked.

"You seem to look alright; I think you should go back to your palace. Your parents must be really worried about you by now." Krome said.

She looked straight into Krome's eyes as she was totally surrendered to his gorgeous appearance and the sweet characteristics of an innocent gentleman. She softly answered him with her lovely smile.

"My father's palace is far from here. It will take more than a day on the horse to get back. It will be difficult for me to walk through the night by myself because now it is almost dark already. Perhaps I will stay here for tonight. How about you, my Guardian Angel? If you want to leave me here, it is alright. Again thank you for saving me from the God of the Snake," Princess Adelia said.

"Would you be afraid with other snakes or other wild beasts? If you are not afraid of them then I will leave you now." Krome politely joked with the princess.

She changed her look suddenly as she would be frightened if Krome decided to leave now. He looked at her face; he knew how she felt. He knew her heart was pure because she was willing to die for the sake of other people and she had no intention to stop him. He told the princess as he pointed to big rock on the top of the mountain.

"We will sleep on that big rock tonight, Princess. It would be safer than down here. . . . I think we should start to climb up there . . . now," Krome said.

Princess Adelia looked at Krome as she tried to tell him that mountain was too high for her to climb. She guessed it probably would take her all night just to climb to the top.

"It will take me all night just to climb up there," Princess Adelia said.

"Hah, hah, hah, hah," Krome laughed.

"Why are you laughing my guardian angel?" Princess Adelia asked.

"If you would not mind I could carry you up there if you don't want to climb," Krome said with his welcome smile.

Princess Adelia put her face down as she felt shy because no man had ever touched her body. She then slowly raised her face to look at Krome and politely answered him with her gratitude.

"Thank you, but I don't want to give you any more trouble; can we just stay here? I think you have done too much for me already," Princess Adelia said.

"Don't be afraid, Princess Adelia, besides I don't want you to smell this ugly smell of the snake's blood all night. I don't really like this smell myself. Please stand up close next to my body and put your arms around my shoulders . . . don't be afraid," Krome told Adelia.

He grabbed her waist and flew straight to the top of the rock on the top of the mountain. She was scared with the height as Krome flew up near the top of the mountain. She held on to his body tighter without notice of her action.

77

As Krome landed on the top of the big rock, Princess Adelia completely relinquished her heart to him as she has never touched any man's body until now. She kept holding on around his shoulders with both arms and looked straight into his eyes.

"We are here . . . Princess Adelia, I think you should look for a comfortable spot to sleep for tonight," Krome kindly reminded her.

She was ashamed of him as she reassured her mind; she softly apologized to Krome.

"I'm really sorry . . . for my irregular behavior, my Guardian Angel," Adelia said.

"Please, just call me Krome; I like Krome better than the words guardian angel. Are you hungry, Princess?" Krome said to the princess.

"No, I'm . . . I'm not really hungry, Krome," Princess Adelia denied.

"I also don't want you to call me Princess. Please just call me Adelia," she said. Krome told the princess to stay on the rock as he quickly flew down to the mountainside.

"I'll be back Adelia, please don't go anywhere," Krome said to Princess Adelia.

Princess Adelia thought Krome was probably upset with the way she acted toward him. She believed maybe he would not come back. She still appreciated his rescue from the snake. A moment later Krome was back with fruits and water for the princess and he gave them to her.

"Adelia, I know you are hungry. Don't be shy, please you must eat these fruits and here is the water for your thirst," Krome told her.

Princess Adelia felt so happy to see Krome return and she thanked him with her grateful attitude for the fruits and water.

"Thank you so much Krome for your kindness. I wish

. . . I could find my prince like you. Please forgive me, for speaking out the truth from my heart," Princess Adelia said.

Krome looked at her innocent beautiful face; he could feel her true love and pure heart she had for him. But as the immortal life filled with the enlightenment, Krome was only delightful with her ecclesiastically spiritual energies. He could leisurely conquer her heart and undesirable mind to feel the same way as he did.

Krome lay down on the big rock next to her closing his eyes to see the other side of the world; he saw his mother was safe with Princess Hollidia. Princess Adelia felt so good after she ate the fruits and drank the water; she turned to look at Krome, she felt very delightful. She reached out her soft pretty hand to touch the gorgeous muscles on his chest and she gave Krome a kiss with her sweetly grateful whisper.

"Thank you for the water and the fruits, my Guardian Angel," She whispered.

She slowly leaned her body down to rest on him; she felt so calm and peaceful, then she started to fall into her sleep. Krome gently touched Princess Adelia's hair as he opened his eyes and looked up into the sky upon the stars and talked inside his mind.

"Aquarus, my task is done here. I will bring her back to her kingdom tomorrow. Her parents will be surprised and grateful for her survival," Krome said.

Krome sensed the faithful energies of the princess were flowing through his body constantly while she was cozily sleeping on his chest. He could read her ingenuous mind; her love was pure as the smooth rhythms of her heartbeat recurred regularly, filled with no temptation, only the enlightenment. She would give her life back to him to repay him for what he had done for her. Krome wanted to get up to meditate but he did not want to disturb Princess Adelia's peace of mind. He let her sleep through the night; he used his spiritual insight to communicate with the princess's mind on the purposes of lives, the lives on this wonderful planet and the will of the God of the Enlightenment.

Princess Adelia slowly opened her eyes as the sun was shining upon her beautiful face in the early morning; she was still on Krome's body. She raised her head with a great smile and greeted Krome.

"Good morning, Krome. It is such a beautiful morning on the top of the mountain. Forgive me . . . that I fell asleep on you. I'm truly gratified to stay by your side. I've never felt this way in my entire life; I feel like I've been touched by an angel," Adelia said.

She then lifted her beautiful body off from Krome and she sat next to him. Krome replied with an encouraging smile as he felt the happiness inside of her heart.

"Good morning Adelia, I hope you had a good sleep last night," Krome said.

"Thank you . . . Krome . . . I . . . ," Princess Adelia said.

"I truly enjoyed seeing you have your life back and you are able to understand the will of God, the light over the darkness," Krome said.

Princess Adelia turned her head to look at Krome as he got up and sat next to her. She was speechless for a moment then she curiously asked him.

"Krome . . . are you a cyberian?" Adelia asked.

"Yes, I am cyberian . . . just like you . . . but I am different," Krome answered.

"If you are one of us . . . why do you possess the power of God?" Adelia continued.

"I've never seen someone like you since I was born.

You make me feel like an angel. I don't think I can ever feel the same way I used to any more after what had happened to me yesterday and last night," Princess Adelia described her feeling.

"What do you mean by 'but I am different'?" Adelia asked.

Krome kept looking at Princess Adelia as he pretended he did not hear what she had asked him as Adelia continued the conversation.

"You don't have to tell me about yourself if you don't want to," Adelia said.

Princess Adelia looked straight into Krome's eyes as she wondered what reason and why Krome suddenly kept quiet and did not want to talk to her.

"But you . . . you are my real angel because no one could ever defeat this most powerful giant snake that has lived for over nine thousand years," Adelia told Krome.

Krome reached out his hand to touch the princess's hair gently as he continued his conversation and tried to explain to her.

"Once I was born in the cyberian form just like you . . . but I have been chosen by God to carry on his will to save good people like you. My family used to have good lives together in a paradise place and now . . . now we are separated and no one else lives there any more. My father was killed not long ago . . . in my time," Krome told Princess Adelia.

Princess Adelia changed the look on her face with grief, as she understood a man like him still suffered from the past with the painful memories.

"This world . . . this world is absolutely beautiful and most comprehensive but yet is still filled with the darkness . . . suffering . . . for what I mean," Adelia said and she continued.

81

"We are the people . . . the part of it; we just want to live in peace and harmony but . . . but sometimes we can't when the light and the darkness collide together," Adelia continued.

Princess Adelia slowly leaned against Krome as she continued talking by herself.

"I was faded in the darkness then I was brought back into light by your rescue. I've never imagined people like you still suffer with the painful memories like me," Adelia said.

Adelia's heart was filled with sympathies for what Krome had gone through and his happy childhood life was turned upside down. She could feel his pains inside of her heart.

"Why, Krome? Or because you have received these powers in the exchange . . . you have to be separated away from your family," Adelia expressed her feeling.

Krome again turned around to look at Princess Adelia's eyes then he turned his face away as he continued telling her about his story.

"No. Not that. . . . This happened after my village had been destroyed and my father was killed. Sometime people want the powers and they are willing to do anything, even to worship the God of Darkness to kill or to destroy the others just to gain their own. For example, it is just like the giant snake, Serpenum; he must eat people like you to become a powerful, immortal snake. If I possessed this kind of power before it happened to my village . . . maybe . . . my family would still live good lives," Krome explained Adelia.

"Now I'm God's destiny; I will lead good people against the force of the darkness. I will collide with the darkness in every corner of the globe and the light will be shining over and dominate on this planet," Krome continued as he looked back at Princess Adelia.

"I am not who you think I am. I'm the force of light, the light within life. I can feel your pain and I can change its course. Do you understand me, Princess Adelia?" Krome said.

"I am not a victim any more; I no longer suffer with these painful feelings so you don't need to feel sorry for me. I wish you could become someone like me so you would be able to understand what I'm talking about. I think you will be safe maybe until the end of your time; you are the purpose of life which is the will of God," Krome showed his true feeling.

Princess Adelia grabbed and held Krome's hands; she felt better after she heard what Krome just told her that he was no longer a victim.

"Where are the rest of your family members, Krome?" Adelia asked.

"My mother and my younger brother have survived; they were captured and were brought back to Almar Kingdom. That place was my parents' birthplace and I have never been there since my birth," Krome told Adelia.

"After I return to my palace, I will ask my parents for permission to allow me to travel with you. I hope you don't mind for me to go along with you," Princess Adelia told Krome.

"Because I always want to see the world outside my kingdom and this way I could serve you as my gratitude to repay you back," Adelia explained.

"It doesn't mean I want to deny your peer; it will be hard for a girl like you to travel a far distance from your palace and beside there are more dangers ahead of us," Krome said.

Princess Adelia turned herself face to face with

Krome and held both of his hands as she kneeled down in front him and explained how she felt about him.

"I believe you could protect me as you have already done that once. I do not feel safe even in my own kingdom as you can feel it too," Princess Adelia said.

"Some Wizards who claimed that they helped to cure and protect people from all harm, worshiped the God of Darkness; the corrupted and dictated leaders who claimed that they served and protect people, usually hungered for the powers to control and suppress the freedom of the people. They both worked side by side; they shared the same interest just to gain their own interests and powers," Princess Adelia explained.

Krome was silent for a moment as he looked upon Princess Adelia's face then he accepted her request with one condition.

"Yes, I will let you come along with me but first you must return to your palace. I think I should bring you back to your palace to see your parents first," Krome told Adelia.

Princess Adelia put her arms around Krome's shoulders as he flew down the mountain and direct to her palace. He decided to get down near the farm where nobody could see him and the princess. Krome told the princess he wanted to take a walk and to see the towns and the city in her kingdom. Samatean was considered the second largest kingdom on the planet, filled with stone buildings, iron structures, museums, shopping centers, town centers and resident homes. Krome used to see it in his visionary but now he saw it with own eyes. He was really amazed how the cyberian world was so like the complex where he once was raised in the jungles and the mountains.

"You could tell all people in your kingdom not to

worry about the snake any more but I could sense someone would be upset if they knew I killed their deity's
snake," Krome said.

Many people including adults and children ran to see
Princess Adelia; they were very surprised that she had
survived this great ordeal. Most of them thought it was a
miracle for her safe return as they followed and shouted
to greet her on the street.

"Long live the Princess, long live the Princess, long
live Princess Adelia. God has blessed your soul, your
highness," The citizens in the Samatean Kingdom
shouted.

Princess Adelia was a popular princess in her kingdom and amongst all the citizens because of her beauty,
kindness, and cares she had toward them. They were
cheerfully following behind her and Krome all the way to
the king's palace. The King, Queen, leaders and soldiers
of Samatean Kingdom were so disturbed by the noisy
crowds; they came out to see what had happened to the
citizens. They were very happy to see Princess Adelia as
she and Krome entered the palace's gate. Princess Adelia
introduced Krome to her parents, the king and queen in
front of the king's palace.

"Father, Mother, this is Krome, the warrior who
saved me from the snake. He defeated and killed the
snake," Princess Adelia told the King and the Queen.

The king and the queen were very happy to see the
princess was safe and the snake was killed. The king announced to the citizens in his kingdom to celebrate the
safe return of his daughter and the defeat of the snake.

"To all citizens in this kingdom, thank God, thank
Krome, the warrior who has saved my daughter's precious life from this great danger and also has saved all of
us from the life threatening situation. Now we can live in

peace and no longer have to sacrifice any life. I order all of you to have the celebration for this victory for our kingdom," the King spoke.

"The celebration starts tomorrow and please make welcome to Krome, the great warrior. Samatean once again will live in peace and the prosperity," the King continued.

"Krome! Krome! Mighty Krome, thank you for saving our kingdom, thank you! Thank you, Krome and long live Princess Adelia," the citizens shouted.

The citizens of Samatean shouted and cheered at Krome as he waved his hands back at them and most young women kept their eyes and their smiles upon him.

"You all are welcome, may the light forever shine upon this kingdom and peace will be always with you. God brings the enlightenment to all of you." Krome said.

Young children, men, and women surrounded Krome as some tried to touch him and the princess, some young women tried to reach to kiss him. Princess Adelia put her arms around Krome's waist and she stood proudly by his side with the great excitement as she saw the reaction and the happiness of the people in her kingdom.

On a distance away a small group of people including some evil Wizards and some bad leaders who had connections with Diron and Valimus were not happy at all; they sensed their dangers were coming. They walked toward Krome as they wanted to find out who he really was. Wizard Mongon, who associated with Diron and held the highest rank in Samatean kingdom, walked toward Krome and spoke to him.

"Welcome to Samatean Krome, the greatest warrior. My name is Mongon; I'm the head of the Wizards in this kingdom. You must be a powerful man; otherwise, you would have never defeated Serpenum, the God of the

Snake. May God forgive you, young warrior. This is the secret creature that belonged to our God," Mongon explained.

Mongon showed his disappointment to Krome and Princess Adelia as he heard the snake was killed. He turned to look at Princess Adelia with his anger and explained to her.

"Princess Adelia, my precious child, you support to save your people and your kingdom but instead he killed the snake and you have brought chaos and doom to this kingdom. You are both disgraceful people." Mongon said.

Then he asked everyone with him to go back to the castle; Mongon discussed the plan to kill Krome and Princess Adelia. Krome tried to comfort Princess Adelia's mind as he put his hand on her shoulder and reassured her feeling.

"Don't worry, Adelia; we will work it out to save your father's kingdom. These are the forces of darkness who love to see you and your kingdom destroyed," Krome said.

The king told his people to return to their homes and invited Krome into his palace. He saw his daughter seemed to be close to Krome then he started to talk to her.

"My precious daughter, God has spared your life by sending this mighty young warrior to save you. My heart filled with tremendous joy and tranquility but I don't know how I can reward this young warrior," the king said.

"I will reward you the most beautiful young woman in my kingdom by your own choice with many gold, lands, and servants," the king said to Krome.

"Your majesty, forgive me for not accepting these gifts. I don't want anything at all; I just came here to save Princess Adelia; I think she deserves to live longer than the giant snake who proclaimed to be the God," Krome told the king.

"Father, my life is saved and brought back by Krome; I was supposed to be gone forever, never to return to see you again. He has not just only saved me but he has saved the whole kingdom. I do not want you to feel that I disobey you, Father. I have already made up my mind. I will give my life to Krome with or without your blessing. He is my guardian angel. Father, if he had not shown up, maybe I would be already inside the snake's belly," Adelia said to her father.

The king agreed with his daughter's decision and he knew this was the truth of her heart that he could not deny it. Without Krome, she would probably already be dead.

"Adelia, my beloved daughter, I have nothing to stop you. This is a reasonable thought but does Krome agree with your decision?" the king asked.

"We will miss you, Adelia. We don't want to lose you again," the queen said.

"Mother, don't worry, I will always come back to see you," Adelia said.

"Yes Father, Krome has promised to protect me. I will follow wherever he goes and thank you for your understanding," Princess Adelia said.

The king turned to discuss with the queen that they should let their daughter marry Krome first before they leave the kingdom. This would be a good gift for Krome since he did not want anything.

"Adelia since you have made up your mind to follow Krome, I would like you to marry him first before you leave this kingdom," the King said.

"Your majesty, I am God's destiny; I travel around the planet to save good people like her. I wish Princess Adelia would change her mind to stay here with you. I will accept her as my traveling companion and to take care of her as my best friend; thus, I cannot marry any woman. Forgive me your majesty; I hope you kindly understand my reason," Krome kneeled down and said in front of the king and queen.

"Yes, I see. I would like to ask both of you to stay here for a few days before you leave. We want Princess Adelia to spend more time with us, as she will be away from our kingdom and me. And where will you go from here, Krome?" the King asked.

"Your majesty, I will go to visit Almar Kingdom because I have some business to take care of over there," Krome said.

The king suddenly talked with his finger pointing up into the air after he heard the word Almar Kingdom.

"Oh! Almar Kingdom . . . that kingdom is our great allied kingdom," the King said.

Mongon stood with his group listening to the king's and Krome's conversations then he heard the word, Almar Kingdom, he soon made an excuse to the King to allow him to return to his wizard castle.

"Your majesty, forgive us. We have something to discuss, besides we would like to leave your majesty and queen alone with Princess Adelia and Krome. This is a family matter, your majesty. Please excuse us," Mongon said.

The king ordered the mates inside the palace to prepare the room for Krome to stay and asked Princess Adelia to show him the room and the palace.

"Adelia you can show Krome around the palace and his room and bring him some clothes too. I think the warrior probably needs to rest and Adelia please take care of Krome for me," the king said.

Mongon went to his wizard castle with his people after he had heard Krome would travel to Almar Kingdom in the next few days. He asked all the leaders who followed him to make a plan to kill Krome and the princess. Mongon used his magic power to put the spell on some of the people in the kingdom. They suddenly became ill with acute pains and pale appearance; their families' members were panicked because of the strange sickness. These incidents were spread over the kingdom and soon were told to the king. Mongon was very clever as he created the chaos in the kingdom and then he put the blame on Krome and Princess Adelia. He explained to the king these were the curses from the God of the Snake, Serpenum, who had lived for thousands of years to protect this land and the people in the kingdom but Krome and Princess Adelia killed him. He explained to the king and queen there was nothing he could do; the only way was to capture Krome and Princess Adelia to make the sacrifice and to ask for forgiveness from the God of the Snake. He had suggested to the king that this sacrifice must be made soon; otherwise, the chaos and doom would happen in the kingdom such as death, war and next would be the king's life.

"Your majesty, this sacrifice is to ask God's forgiveness that we have destroyed the secret animal, God of the Snake who has protected our kingdom for thousands of years. In the return only one life every one hundred years but now Krome killed the secret snake that belonged to God. Now God is very angry and punishes our people and the kingdom . . . it will also affect your majesty's life too . . . be wise my king," Mongon said.

The king totally agreed with Mongon about the curse and the new threat. The king granted Mongon the power to do whatever necessary to bring back the peace to his people.

"Your majesty, Krome and Princess Adelia should be

killed for this sacrifice; two lives for a life, God Serpenum's life. Krome should never kill the snake. If we want to kill God Serpenum, we could have done it by ourselves a long time ago but we think about the safety and future of this kingdom," Mongon continued.

The king asked Wizard Mongon and his people to handle this matter and even secretly approved him to capture Krome and Princess Adelia when they were on their trip to Almar outside the city to sacrifice for the loss of God Serpenum's soul. Mongon ordered all of his leaders of the armies to assemble all the best warriors in the whole kingdom and prepared the traps to capture Krome on the route between Samatean and Almar. Mongon suspected Krome was a holy child who Diron searched for ten years ago. He told the soldiers to build the sacrificing site next to the road on the mountainside. He stood and looked from the top of the mountain and whispered in his mind with regret of the loss of the God of Snake.

"Even if you have wings and nine lives; you will not escape these deadly traps. A life is for a life, Krome. You are the enemy of our God, you must be destroyed," Mongon said.

Mongon and his people walked around the area to make sure no one would be aware of their deadly traps.

Back in the Princess Adelia's palace Krome sat down in his meditation on the bed seeing all the actions of Mongon's people; he even knew the mind of the king. He would solve it once and for all when he passed through Mongon's sacrificing site. Krome opened his eyes as Princess Adelia entered through the door of his room.

"How is your mother, Adelia?" Krome asked.

"She is disappointed with my decision but she thinks it is better than to let me die by the snake. She only prays for me to be safe wherever I go," Adelia said.

"I have something I want to tell you. Please close that door and come here," Krome said.

"What is it, Krome?" Adelia asked.

"Remember Wizard Mongon? He put the spell on some of the people so they could become sick. With this trick he told the King that Serpenum has cursed your kingdom. Now the King believes him and Mongon plans to capture and sacrifice us to revenge Serpenum's soul. The king already knows about this plan; he agrees and grants Mongon the absolute power to kill you and me," Krome explained to Adelia.

Princess Adelia was very angry with her father's weakness; she wanted to see him at once but Krome told her to calm down. He knew nothing could change the King's mind as he once had already allowed Adelia to die in the sacrifice to the snake.

"You must calm down Adelia, I know what to do. It is not your father's fault; he is tricked and blinded by Mongon's wizard power. Mongon is the force of darkness, sooner or later I will face him face to face. He worships the God of the Snake, Serpenum, and he must kill me for revenge . . . he will do whatever he can," Krome said.

Krome stood up and walked to the window and looked down upon the hillside from the castle and continued his conversation with Princess Adelia.

"You're right, Adelia. The world is absolutely beautiful and yet it fills with darkness, I mean these bad people, the evil forms in the cyberian forms," Krome said.

Princess Adelia walked close behind Krome and she put her arms around his waist then leaned her head against his back. She spoke softly as she revealed her true feeling to him.

"I realize my life does not belong here. I believe God

has sent you to save me, if not my life would be already perished," Adelia said then breathed her deep breath.

"I feel secure and free every time I am with you; I rather die by your side than stay here. I feel my life is complete when I am close to you; I just don't want anything else. I want to leave this place as soon as possible, Krome," Princess Adelia said.

Her tears flowed down her face as she walked to the other side of the window away from Krome. She felt worse than ever after she knew about her father's misunderstanding and Mongon's evil plan to destroy her life again and again.

Four days had passed by; Krome and Princess Adelia were ready to leave. The king and the queen accompanied their daughter and Krome to the gate of the palace. The king had ordered one of the guards to bring a gorgeous white horse, sword, food and water to give it to his daughter. The queen was speechless as she already knew what would happen to her daughter and Krome. She only cried and wasted her tears away because there was nothing she could do to stop this madness. She thought this would be the purpose of her daughter's life even though she once was saved by Krome. She only could pray to God and let him decide her daughter's destiny. Princess Adelia talked to her mother as she tried to comfort the queen not to worry about her.

"Mother, don't worry, Krome will protect me from all harm. Someday I will return to see you and Father again . . . Krome and I will be back for sure," Princess Adelia said.

She went to give her mother the last hug and kiss then she turned to look at her father for a moment before she started to say something to him.

"Father, I will return and please take good care of yourself and Mother," Adelia said.

The king replied with his shame as he tried to hide something from her and Krome.

"I wish your journey with safety and happiness, Adelia . . . my princess," The king said.

Krome bowed and spoke to the king with his confidence.

"Your majesty, I promise to bring Princess Adelia back," Krome said.

He lifted Princess Adelia up to help her to get on the horseback. She dressed herself like a woman warrior because she knew the road ahead was not likely to be easy for her. She moved the horse close to her mother and gave her a last kiss; she turned around to her father and did the same thing.

"Good-bye, Father, good-bye, Mother, I promise I will return. Take care," Adelia said.

"Your majesty, good-bye, we will return safely," Krome said.

He pulled the rope and walked in front of the horse waving good-bye to the king, the queen, and citizens of Samatean.

"Long live Princess Adelia, long live Mighty Krome!" they shouted back at the princess and Krome.

Now Krome and Princess Adelia were far away from the palace after they had traveled almost half of the day. The sun was overhead and the reflecting heat from the ground was hot. Krome knew Princess Adelia was tired and she should take a rest.

"How are you, Adelia? I think the weather is too hot for you," Krome asked.

"I am fine . . . thank you, Krome," Adelia replied.

"I think you should take a rest under that tree for a

while. The heat of the sun seems to be hot for you to continue on . . . we can resume our journey later this afternoon," Krome said.

He pulled the horse rope along with him and walked toward the big tree. Krome had walked all the way to here and Princess Adelia looked at him; she wondered why Krome looked so clean like he had done nothing at all.

"Are you tired, Krome? This is a long walk for you . . . I think you should be more tired than me," Adelia said.

"No, I'm not tired at all, Adelia . . . please do not worry about me," Krome answered.

Princess Adelia took the sack of water from the back of the horse and she asked Krome if he would want to drink it. Again Adelia kept looking at Krome as she tried to say some things to him.

"Looks like you did not do anything at all, no sweat, no dust; your body always looks clean. How do you do that Krome?" Adelia wondered as she asked Krome.

Krome turned around and looked at Adelia for a moment with his big smile before he began to answer her question.

"I am not who you think who I am. I am different . . . Adelia . . . remember?" Krome said.

Princess Adelia got down from the horse and drank water from the sack. She walked around Krome and looked at him from the head to toe and then she asked him again.

"Would you like to drink the water? Please drink it," Adelia said.

"No, I don't feel thirsty and thank you for asking . . . Adelia," Krome answered.

"I seem to recognize that you haven't eaten or drank since we met," Adelia continued.

"You don't need anything when you possess the

power of God. Your life is just like the light, you will not get old nor will you die. You are the nature, the physical universe; you are immortal," Krome explained.

"So will you live forever without eating or drinking, Krome?" Adelia said.

"No . . . not forever," Krome said.

"Wait. . . . I don't really understand, first you say you will not die then when I ask . . . you answer that is not forever. I'm sorry that I'm so confused," Adelia said.

"That's why I wish you to become someone, just like me and then you will understand what I try to tell you . . . Adelia . . . your highness . . . I mean." Krome tried to joke with Adelia.

Princess Adelia wondered if Krome possessed the power of God, he probably could do anything that he wanted.

"Could you bring people back to life from death?" Adelia again asked.

"No, there are some things I could not do. I can cure all the sickness and prevent lives from catastrophic conditions but I can't bring the dead back to life. Another thing is to change people's minds, I can't change people's mind but I can show them between right and wrong, good and bad, light and darkness. Even God himself could not control people's minds and desires; people can desire with their own faith. They will be good if they believe in good; they will be bad if they practice their faith with bad purpose. Thus, there will be always good and bad people on this planet," Krome explained.

"I think . . . I asked you too many questions already . . . I'm sorry, Krome," Adelia said.

"How are you doing now? I think we should move on, Adelia," Krome said.

"I feel fine now and thank you for explaining to me all these things," Adelia said.

Krome helped Adelia to get up on the horse then he pulled the horse rope and walked backed to the road. Adelia did not want Krome to walk and she asked him to ride on the horse with her.

"I don't want you to walk; please you can ride this horse with me, Krome," Adelia said.

Krome already knew that Princess Adelia always wanted to be very close to him but he pretended not to recognize her feeling as he kept saying the opposite.

"I think you would be uncomfortable if I ride with you," Krome answered.

"No . . . I don't mind. I feel the opposite of what you've thought," Adelia said.

"I agree with you . . . this will make our pace faster," Krome said.

Krome jumped and sat on the horse behind Adelia. They rode the horse faster and faster as they got closer to the place where Mongon's people were waiting to trap them. Krome used his supernatural power to help the horse to move along faster and Princess Adelia felt more comfortable as she leaned her back against Krome's body. She came to realize that surrounding his body, the energies and atmosphere were so balanced. It was not just her body but she could see the horse too; the horse was so consistent with its energy. Each stroke and each pace, the horse moved faster and seemed to be weariless. She knew this must be Krome's power and his surrounding energies. She was happy that Krome treated her like someone special and very close to him. She always felt this way every time she touched him; her mind was calm and peaceful. She did not even feel hungry or thirsty on this long ride; she believed Krome was an angel and she thought she could never ask for anything else more than to be close to him. Krome rode the horse with his both eyes closed and could see all the actions of Mongon's people ahead of him. Princess Adelia turned her face back to look at Krome; she wondered why Krome kept his eyes closed but she did not want to disturb him. A few hours later she turned to look at him again and he still closed his eyes; with an odd feeling and curiosity she decided to ask him.

"Why do you keep your eyes closed, Krome? I've never seen anyone ride a horse with both eyes closed all the time like you. Can you see the road?" Adelia said.

"Adelia, I don't need to see the road in front of me and with my eyes closed I can see not just in front of us but I can see thousands of miles away. Just relax and don't worry . . . and just enjoy your ride," Krome answered without opening his eyes.

She felt completely confident with his supernatural capability; she thought he was totally different from all cyberians. Adelia thought she had made the right decision to follow Krome's footsteps as she could see his gentleness, his immaterial essence, his honesty, and the way he treated her with respect. She knew she could trust him more than anybody on this planet.

8

Princess Adelia Becomes a Woman Warrior

The long ride from Samatean palace was worth the great experience of the naturally magnificent wilderness for Princess Adelia as they passed through the peacefully isolated region that was a feature by the mountains, the tropical evergreen trees, green hills, and extraordinary lakes. The sun was down almost on the top of the far distant forest on the west horizon; Krome decided to find a place for the princess to rest for the night. He rode the horse to the lake near a small hill away from the road as he explained to Adelia.

"We will rest here tonight, this is a safe spot where you can swim or wash yourself here in this lake," Krome said.

The beautiful lake of this region was offset by the vast tranquil waters and filled with various colorful aquatic plants. Krome stopped the horse nearby the sand and the rock on the lake's shore then he let the horse loose. The horse moved to drink the water and ate the grass on the green hill a distance from him. He moved to sit on the rock and started his meditation. Princess Adelia gave Krome a kiss on his cheek and watched him as he sat quietly in his meditation. She started to feel a little hungry and walked toward the horse and took out some dried foods and came back to sit by his side again. Krome opened his eyes and looked at Princess Adelia; he wanted to train her to use the sword to protect herself when he was not around. Then he told her what would happen tomorrow and asked her.

"Adelia we will pass Mongon's people by the midday tomorrow on this road across those mountains. Mongon had his soldiers prepare traps and the sacrificing site on top of that mountain as they plan to capture you and me to sacrifice to the God of Darkness. We could avoid this collision but I want to stop them before they destroy your father's kingdom. Do you know how to use that sword? I know the sword on the horseback must be yours . . . it will be good if you know how use it," Krome said.

"No, I've never held or used the sword to fight with anyone in my entire life. I was not allowed to touch it around my palace," Princess Adelia said.

"I want to teach you how to use the sword to defend yourself in case anyone wants to hurt you when you are not around me. Finish your food first," Krome said.

Princess Adelia finished the last piece of the food while Krome went to bring her sword from the horseback. He put his sword down on the rock next to Princess Adelia and he drew out her sword. He looked at the sword and spun it like a fan around his body and he made the attacking and defending moves to show the princess.

"It is very light and is shorter than Aquarus's sword but it will be good for you to practice with, Adelia," Krome said.

"Are you ready to begin your practicing, Adelia? If you are, then come here and hold the sword like this," Krome showed Adelia.

Princess Adelia got off the rock and walked to Krome

to take the sword from him. She then almost dropped it from her hand as she thought the sword was lighter.

"It is too heavy for me, Krome but the way you hold it like you hold nothing. It will take me a while to get used to its weight," Adelia said.

He went to pick up the Aquarus sword on the rock and jumped into the air and he landed next to her.

"First you must watch my moves carefully, this is called the attacking move and you slash the sword up and down like this as you step forward each step. Then this is called the defending move, you must swing your sword like this against your opponent's sword," Krome said.

"Krome, I don't . . . I don't think I can do this," Adelia said.

"You almost get all the moves, Adelia; you learn fast and keep going," Krome tried to encourage the princess as she struggled with the sword. He jumped back to sit on the rock and closed his eyes to meditate again.

Princess Adelia held on to the sword and looked at Krome. She really wanted to give up her practice but Krome told her to keep focusing with her mind and strength with his eyes were closed.

"Adelia keep concentrating with your energy and your mind. You will overcome the difficulty and the weight of the sword," Krome said.

She wondered that Krome probably must see all parts of her body when she took a swim; even with his eyes closed, he still could see everything around him.

"You must not think of anything else or you will never learn these skills to protect yourself. I could see beyond your thought and could feel what you feel. You must concentrate with this practice," Krome interrupted Adelia's thinking.

Adelia lifted the sword up with her two soft hands

and followed Krome's advice. She suddenly felt her strength and energy surrounding her body change dramatically. She could see her ability and was able do all the moves that Krome just showed her. The harder she tried the better she got. Krome kept penetrating his supernatural power within Princess Adelia's energies and further showed her in her vision many complex skills. She was so amazed and interested with all the actions and techniques she had just learned. Adelia gained her inner powers gradually as Krome slowly withdrew his assisted energy from her body. Her energies somehow were compatible with Krome and easily emerged on her own because her spirit and body were pure as she had never been touched or disturbed by any man. She now felt completely confident with herself and quickly improved her great ability more than she could imagine. She felt the sword getting lighter and was even able just to hold it with one hand. She swung the sword around just like Krome did and at the same time she spun her body into the air higher. Throughout this process Krome had taught Princess Adelia how to control, use and improve her strength and energies surrounding her body. She finally mastered the fighting skills and energized her strength as she lifted her body and flipped it in the air with her own powers. Adelia could not believe herself; she knew this power must come from Krome.

"Is it from you, Krome? I could not believe that I could do this thing in just a few hours," Princess Adelia said.

Krome opened his eyes to look at Adelia as he completely withdrew all his energy back into his body.

"No not mine. This is your own power, Adelia. From the beginning I've showed and helped you to find all the channels of your strengths and energies, then when you have discovered and gained it, I slowly drew all my energy back from your mind and body. All these moves and strength are yours," Krome told Adelia.

Princess Adelia was so happy that she had learned not just the skills of the sword but she had also learned how to use and control her own potential energies.

Krome knew Princess Adelia was able to defend herself with her sword against many regular soldiers at a time. He wanted her to have a real feel in the real fight and asked her to test her skill and strength with him.

"Are you ready to feel the real fight, Adelia? I will let you test your skills and your strength with me. Don't be afraid; you will not get hurt in this fight," Krome said.

Adelia was afraid that she would hurt Krome if she fought harder with her sword.

"You must use it as if you are in the real fight to protect your life and don't worry about me, I never get hurt, ready? Go!" Krome asked Adelia to fight the hardest she could.

Krome used his dagger and cyberian strength to fight with Princess Adelia. She jumped and flipped her body into the air then she flew directly toward him with the sword in her hand. She constantly attacked him with the blade of her sword and Krome could feel the strength of her sword slashing against his dagger as he could see the spark each time the two blades collided. She did the best in both ways, the attacking and defending movements; she even lifted herself into the air fighting with Krome face to face like a mighty warrior. She was truly proud of her capability and she asked Krome to use Aquarus's sword to fight with her.

"Krome, why don't you use that long sword with me?" Adelia asked.

"That sword is too heavy for you. I think you have learned enough for today and now you should wash yourself and be ready to take a rest for tonight, Adelia," Krome said.

Krome and Princess Adelia jumped back up to the rock. He sat down as the princess put the sword back into the shield. She walked close to Aquarus's sword and tried to pick it up; she could not lift it at all. She was surprised with the weight of the sword.

"This must be the sword of God, Krome. I see you carry this sword like you carry the weight of the wooden stick. I've not realized it is very heavy like this," Adelia said.

Princess Adelia felt a little bit tired and dirty on her body from the sweat; she decided to take a bath and have a swim in this crystal clear water. She took off her short leather jacket and walked into the water with her silky underwear. She just passed her seventeenth birthday not long ago and her body was medium, which was perfectly matched with her height, five feet and nine. Her light pinkish white skin on her face was softly smooth and her innocent blue eyes were as lovely as her light red lips. She let her light brown hair down, covering her shoulders. Considering her beauty and the shape of her body, resembled the appearance of the goddess child, it was easy to comprehend that she had truly possessed her feminine virginity. Her silky long legs were as beautiful as her firmly thin abdomen. Princess Adelia was the absolutely beautiful, young woman in the entire planet. She relaxingly swam next to the rock where Krome sat and asked him to join her in the water.

"Do you want to swim with me, Krome? Come on Krome, the water is very clean and fun to swim . . . it is so cool," Adelia invited Krome.

"Go ahead, Adelia, I am already clean. You just enjoy

yourself and thank you for asking me to swim with you," Krome said.

Krome answered Adelia with both of his eyes closed as he concentrated his spiritual power to keep all the creatures in the lake away from her. After a while she got out of the water and she stood not far from Krome to dry her wet body and her hair. Her irresistible beauty aroused adoration that men would die for. Then she dressed back into her clothes and walked to sit next to him. She looked at Krome's face with her curious mind, then she started to tease him again.

"I see you really don't need anything. Your body even looks more clean than mine; it is not fair . . . Krome, I just took a bath," Adelia complained.

Krome told Princess Adelia that he would continue his meditation through the night so she should find a spot for her to sleep for the night.

"Adelia, I will be in my meditation through the night. I think you should find a comfortable spot to sleep for tonight," Krome said.

She looked around and it seemed could not find any spot on the rock; she decided to sit down back-to-back and leaned against Krome.

"Forgive me, Krome; I don't want to sleep on the rock by myself. When I am close to your body, I can rest with tranquility," Adelia said.

Krome did not reply to her; he knew this would be good for Princess Adelia. Her strengths and energies would grow stronger when her body made contact with him.

She started to meditate like Krome and later that night she had reached the stage which she could be able to perpetuate transmigration and determine her destiny in the next existence of her enchanting inner light, the supernatural power.

The spiritual phenomena shaped into the source of energies by wind, water, rock, trees, planet, moons, and stars surrounding Krome and Princess Adelia as now their energies were strongly combined and faithfully flowed as one with perfect balances between man and woman, just like the forces of yin and yang. They sat back-to-back silently with their true spirits beyond the diversity of their cyberian forms. Princess Adelia thought that she had never experienced something like this; she truly sensed the universally dominant effect in Krome's mind, the delightfulness of the nature, the enlightenment. She comprehended the binding force of light inside of him was as strong as the force that was holding the entire universe together. She realized why he had always treated her the same way since the first day she met him. Princess Adelia had also learned the purpose of lives, the existence of every life form under the force of light; without the force of light, life would never exist. She finally understood Krome's explanations; he used to explain to her that he was the force of light. She thought he had saved her because he protected her life from being destroyed by the force of darkness. Throughout this process Princess Adelia gained not just her great energies and strengths; she also had gained her life's extension, she would live longer than regular cyberians. Her beauty transformed close to the appearance of the angel just like Krome did. Krome was delightful as he knew that Princess Adelia had found her existence inside his heart. He knew this was God's destination to bring Princess Adelia by his side. She now became the force of light close to him; even she was not immortal but her life form was above the cyberian life.

Through the animating principles of life and enlightening journey Princess Adelia had transformed into a completely different life form with mighty strength ranked second after Krome. A whole night passed by like a minute for Krome and Princess Adelia. They opened their eyes as the sunlight of the early morning shone upon their face.

"Good morning, Adelia; how are you feeling? I hope you had a good journey last night. Your body looks much better as your strength gets stronger," Krome said.

"Krome, thank you for the converting energy and the transformation, now I understand you and the meaning of the God of the Enlightenment completely," Adelia said.

She reached down to pick up Aquarus's sword with one hand and handed it to Krome while her other hand held her own sword.

"I can see you have gained your mighty strength and now you are no longer the victim. You are one of the forces of light . . . Congratulation Adelia!" Krome said.

"Yes, I can feel my energy, Krome. Thank you, my guardian angel," Adelia said.

Princess Adelia walked to Krome; she put her arm around his neck and gave him a kiss for what he had done for her. She felt like a princess who finally found a perfect prince.

"I think we should move on, Adelia," Krome said.

"Yes Krome, I sense your mother's danger is coming," Adelia said.

Adelia jumped on horseback, then Krome followed her. She leaned her back on Krome as the horse moved faster and faster in the speed of wind along the road. Now Princess Adelia and Krome became an undivided couple as the transformation of their energies had combined into a single energy source with a perfect equilibrium. Adelia even felt closer to Krome than she had ever been.

9

Adelia versus Mongon

Krome and Adelia rode up along the passages of the mountains closer to Mongon's people. Adelia and Krome controlled their energy sources to lift themselves and the
horse into the air and flew over the traps to the other side
of the road and stopped the horse. Mongon and his soldiers
were amazed when they saw that; then they came out from
their hideout. Mongon laughed to reassure himself as he
floated into the air and landed in front of Krome and
Adelia. He pointed up to his bowmen on the higher spot of
the mountainside aiming the arrows at Krome and Adelia.

"Even if you have nine lives and four wings, you will
never escape this," Mongon said.

"Well we will find about that, Mongon," Adelia said.

"For the sake of heaven, you both must surrender
yourselves to me," Mongon asked Princess Adelia and
Krome to surrender to him.

"Mongon, you still have a chance to change your evil
ways," Krome said.

"Krome, if you don't want to see Princess Adelia get
hurt, you must surrender your soul to me then I will spare
her life," Mongon said to Krome.

"Why don't you ask Princess Adelia? What you
should do to make her change her mind to spare your
lives," Krome replied.

"I know sometimes people make mistakes in their lives with or without their own consciousness but if they admit that they were wrong and make the change to correct their mistake they will be forgiven. Again, I ask all of you to make a right choice so you shall be forgiven." Princess Adelia told all the soldiers who followed Mongon.

"Adelia, what is your competence to make a demand to us, particularly on myself? You are a foolish child . . . don't you know that?" Mongon asked Adelia.

"Wizard Mongon, I will use my ability to solve this matter," Adelia said.

"Hah, hah, hah, hah, hah . . . Hem, you . . . you are truly foolish child, your power to defeat me. Please try your very best . . . my little princess," Mongon laughed and said.

Mongon laughed at Adelia's answer, as he did not realize she now possessed the power, which he could never imagine. He felt more confident with his wizard powers to defeat Krome and Adelia because when Serpenum, the snake, died, it transferred all its powers into Mongon's body so he could take revenge for his soul.

"Krome destroyed the snake to save our kingdom, you all should be proud to live with peaceful lives. Who chooses to be on my side and listen to my words, I shall spare your lives," Adelia said to the soldiers who were ready to fight with her.

"It will not bring the chaos or doom like Mongon who has made up the curses to blind your minds. Please I ask you again to believe in me as I once was your Princess," she said.

"Don't believe this disgraceful child, you should die in the flame of fire to repay God Scrpenum's life that he has destroyed," Mongon angrily shouted at Adelia.

Princess Adelia lifted her body into the air like a sor-

109

cerer and flew toward Mongon then she landed in front of him. She looked straight into his eyes and convinced him not to fight with Krome and her. Mongon was very impressed with Princess Adelia's magical capability but he guessed his wizard and Serpenum's powers would be dominant to any cyberian powers. Krome sat still on the back of the horse watching the scene as he could feel the strong energy from Mongon's dark spiritual power. Suddenly Mongon used his unseen force to lift a big piece of the rock to throw at Adelia as a reflection; she quickly jumped higher in the air and pushed it back to him with her cosmic energy. The two forces collided, causing the rock to explode like dynamite at an equal distance between Adelia and Mongon. Mongon again projected a ball of a very strong energy directly to Princess Adelia; she was swiftly pushed backward as she tried to block that force leaving two big straight tracks on the ground as her two feet moved and pushed into the ground. Adelia could feel the energy pass through her body but Krome rapidly concentrated his cosmic power to help her to assimilate Mongon's dark energy and convert it to her own energy. With that capability, Adelia could transform her body into a transducer and fired back the converted energy at Mongon. Mongon was hit hard by the energized force from Adelia; his body was flipped into the air as he was spun backward a few hundred yards from the position where he previously stood. Mongon truly admired Princess Adelia's creditability and her strength that she was able to reverse his dark energy. Mongon cleverly ordered his twelve strongest warriors to attack and distract Princess Adelia so she would lose her focus on the spiritual energy then it would be a good opportunity for him to kill her.

Krome flew from the back of the horse and landed next to Adelia. He handed her Aquarus's sword and explained to her she must use this sword to cut Mongon's head and it was the only way that she could defeat him. Adelia held the sword with both of her hands lifting it straight into the air above her head as she tried to withdraw all energies surrounding her. With a single strike, Adelia brought all the warriors down to their knees and emptied their strength and they died instantly. She then jumped and landed before Mongon but he moved away from her. Mongon ordered his best archers to shoot the arrows at Princess Adelia and in the same moment she lifted her body higher from the ground and spun around like a tornado and caught all the arrows then threw them back to those soldiers. The arrows impelled through the air and hit all those soldiers who shot the arrows at her. Mongon withdrew his sword and held it with his two hands moving from right to left across his chest as he tried to absorb the energies around him and get ready to strike Adelia. He flew fast and straight and aimed his sword at her heart but he was still slower than Princess Adelia. She swung Aquarus's mighty sword to gain momentum and combined with her cosmic power she directly propelled her blade against Mongon's sword. The two blades collided against each other creating the lightening spark like two electrical cables (negative and positive) touching each other. The battle between Adelia and Mongon was going on for an hour. From the beginning, Mongon's power seemed to be stronger than Adelia, but as the battle went on Adelia kept gaining energies far better than him. Adelia finally brought Mongon down to his knees with her mighty slash as his sword flew off from his hands.

"Mongon, you are the force of darkness; you have poisoned my father's mind and try to kill Krome and me. Today your life will end under Aquarus's sword and you will be surely joined with the darkness forever," Adelia said.

"Please, Princess Adelia, forgive me, please don't kill me and I . . . I know that I have made mistakes because of the snake. Please spare my life, your highness," Mongon begged.

Adelia did not answer him and she turned around and walked toward Krome. Mongon, the snake head and the force of darkness, picked up the sword and ran straight to stab her from the back but Adelia spun herself around faster than Mongon could think and she slashed through his neck. His head fell off his body and rolled around on the ground while his body fell down on his knees with one arm holding onto his sword.

"This one is for the sake of my kingdom and the God of the Enlightenment. Mongon, you would never change," Adelia said.

The rest of the soldiers dropped their swords and bows; they ran toward the princess and kneeled down in front of her and begged her for forgiveness and to spare their lives. Princess Adelia told all the soldiers to return to her kingdom and to be honest with her father and his kingdom.

"All of you must remember, you must go back and never think to betray the king or try to destroy the kingdom. I, Princess Adelia, promise to come back to protect my kingdom and to bring those who are against the kingdom to justice. You must bring this message back and tell everyone in the kingdom . . . be honest with your king," Adelia said to soldiers.

The soldiers were so pleased and happy because Princess Adelia spared their lives. They worshiped her like a God and she told them to burn Mongon's body and his head at the sacrificing site along with all his best men who fought against her. The rest of the soldiers decided to go back to Samatean Kingdom at once. Krome walked close to Princess Adelia and stood by her side to congratulate her on her victory.

"Congratulations Adelia, you now have become the great warrior and the force of light. Your power succeeded the wizard's capability and your strength is equal to one hundred mighty warriors but you must remember that you only use these powers with the good purpose. You must use your wisdom and judgment wisely; you only kill who like to kill the others . . . and serve only the God of the Enlightenment," Krome said.

"Thank you Krome, you helped me to save my father's kingdom. Without you, my life would be already destroyed by the darkness and I will always remember this . . . I'm a part of you. Your determinacy is my destiny," Princess Adelia said.

Princess Adelia recognized Aquarus's sword had no bloodstain at all; she had also remembered not seeing any drop of blood after Krome killed the giant snake. She felt better and safe for her father and his kingdom; she looked at the blade of Aquarus's sword and she turned around to explain to Krome.

"This is like a magic sword; there is no blood, not even a single drop on it. The blood of the dark force could never stain the blade of God's mighty sword," Adelia said.

"This sword belonged to Aquarus, the greatest warrior who always defended the truth and the good people. When Aquarus left this world, his soul became the Holy Spirit. He passed this sword on to me as the gift of honor," Krome said.

"We are better to keep moving on, Adelia. It will take us many more days to reach the shore by this horse then we need to cross the ocean to reach Almar Kingdom," Krome said.

Across the vast mountain ranges and abundant jungles Krome and Adelia traveled days and nights then they finally had arrived at the ocean shore.

"How can we cross the ocean, Krome? There are no ships around," Adelia asked.

Krome jumped off from the horse and did not answer Adelia. He walked up on the rock on the shore and looked into the sea.

"We can ask the giant white whale to help us cross this ocean to the other side or we could wait for the next ship to arrive," Krome answered.

Adelia got off from the horseback and walked to Krome; she put both of her arms around Krome's waist as she stood against his body and looked at the great sea.

"The ocean is so great and so pure with the breezy wind. Standing here we are so tiny and God created this water to support all life forms on the planet. Sometimes people think they are the greatest of all when they possess the power to lead the others. They do not see the beauty of nature and these great purposes," Adelia said.

"But we . . . we are different, even we possess the power of God; we respect every living thing and still feel tiny as we compare us to the universe." Krome made a compliment.

"If all people on this planet truly understand the purpose of lives and the God of the Enlightenment, they will live in the harmony and peace," Adelia said.

"Then there will be no more war, no killing, and no forces of darkness," Krome said.

10

Great White Whales and Sea Monsters

The magnificently colorful landscape of the rocky and sandy beaches offered great opportunities for meditation as Krome and Adelia sat quietly on the giant rock next to spectacular, gorgeous cliff formations to enjoy the pure energies that came from the great ocean. They meditated and combined their spiritual energies to navigate under the crystal bright shallows of the marine world over the grandeur of coral gardens that filled the colorful coral reefs, the green giant seaweeds, and full of the marine creatures then deep into the sea water in the search for the great white whales. Not for long they spotted a pair of great white whales in the water far away and they had used their spiritual powers to communicate with the whales to come to the shore to help them to cross the ocean. The giant whales swam up to the surface of the ocean to meet Krome and Princess Adelia and the whales agreed to help them get to the other side. The male great white whale lifted its body almost half from the water and swam toward the deepest cliff next to the rock where Krome, Adelia, and the horse stood by. The giant white whale was so huge, like the size of a big sailing ship. Krome, Adelia, and the horse got on the back of the whale and they rode on the whale across the ocean. The horse lay down on the back of the whale next to Adelia and Krome as they sat down to enjoy the ride through the cool breeze of the sea. Adelia sat in front of Krome and leaned her back against his chest. She felt very amazed how great the waves and the size of the ocean were when she was actually in the seawater for the first time. They both were quiet for quite a while because this was the first time that they both had experienced the trip across the sea. They were in the middle of the ocean; they could not see any islands around. They had ridden on the whale for more than nine days and now they had reached one of the big islands where there were only the existences of the wild lives, various tropical plants, and jungles. Krome asked the great white whale to rest nearby the island as he and Adelia took the horse to the shore to explore the island.

The sea monster known as the Devil of the Sea, named Osinea, had lived on the deepest ocean floor for many millions of years. Osinea was immortal just like Krome and also possessed the power of God because many millions ago he had eaten the immortal fruits from the Oradius. Thus, he had done many bad things in his entire life, then he had transformed into the sea monster. He destroyed too many lives and was against the God of the Enlightenment; he was stocked in darkness under deepest ocean where there was no light. Every three thousand years only at night he came up to the surface of the sea to capture his prey, as he would consume a million sea creatures and many thousands of the cyberian souls. His body was hard like a rock, even the lava from the volcano would not hurt him and his size was bigger than a three-square-mile island. His legend scared all the people who lived along the coastline and who traveled across the sea.

Mongon sent out the messages with the pigeons to Diron and many other wizards before he was killed to inform them that a young warrior named Krome had destroyed Serpenum, the God of Snake. As the leader of the circle of darkness, Diron asked all the wizards who followed the God of Darkness to meet with him on the Soulless Mountain to perform the ceremony to awake the sea monster to destroy Krome and Princess Adelia. Under the dark sky in the night without the moon, Drion sat in the circle with many other wizards and spelled out the magic words to communicate with the God of the Darkness to awake the sea monster. They informed Osinea, the Devil of the Sea, about the death of the God of the Snake and the rise of the mighty young warrior named Krome.

"In the name of the God of the Dark World, we ask you, the mighty darkness, to awake the Devil of the Sea at once as now the young warrior, the holy child, has arisen to destroy us and disturb your world. You must awake the Devil of the Sea," they prayed.

The strong wind suddenly swirled around them as the response from the God of the Darkness answered to their prayers. Many miles beneath the ocean in the cave of darkness, the sea monster slowly opened his eyes as he acknowledged the message from the God of the Darkness. Osinea yawned and opened his jaw full of sharp fangs and teeth; the air from his mouth created the tsunami waves on the surface of the ocean above him. As he moved out from the cave, the ground was cracked open and triggered a big earthquake thousand miles away. The Devil of the Sea slept for the entire three thousand years and was buried by sand, dirt, rock, and lava over his body so his body was attached to the outermost solid layer of the planet, known as the crust. Each time Osinea shook and broke his body free from the crust, he created the natural disasters along the coastline. The sea monster swam up to the surface of the water and his movement created more tsunami waves. At the surface of the sea he took a deep breath in and let it out; the air that came out of his nose blew the wind into a huge hurricane. The calmness of the ocean turned into violent weather which disturbed the half of the southern hemisphere with hurricanes, storms, floods, and earthquakes as the Devil of the Sea swam and played with ocean water after the three thousand years of his sleep. Osinea now sensed Krome and Princess Adelia a few hundreds miles away and he started to turn his body around and swam toward the island where they were.

Krome and Adelia experienced the worst severe weather as the tsunamis, the serial earthquakes, the hurricanes, and the storms passed through the island. They took the horse to the big cave near the top of the mountain on the island and decided to stay in there for the night. Krome and Adelia sat on the rock back-to-back inside the cave to meditate; they saw what had happened as the Devil of the Sea had awakened.

"Adelia, we will face the battle with the Devil of the Sea soon," Krome said.

"Osinea is very powerful Krome, he created all these disasters," Adelia said.

"Will we be able to defeat him with the powers we have?" Adelia asked.

"Yes we may, the force of the light always dominates the darkness," Krome said.

"We need to be ready for this; we need to combine our energies," Krome told Adelia.

Krome and Adelia went outside the cave to get ready for the battle with the Devil of the Sea as they stood and waited for him on the big rock on the cliff formation in the stormy night on the island. Osinea's body was huge like the size of the island and his shape like a giant rock fish. As he slowly approached the island, he whipped his tail to create the biggest wave to hit the island as he tried to get the attention from Krome and Adelia. Krome and Adelia floated their bodies into the air and flew directly toward the Devil of the Sea.

"Devil of the Sea, we demand you to go back to the bottom of the ocean and calm down all these harmful weathers or your life will end today," Krome said.

"Hoh, hoh, hoh . . . the holy child . . . let's see how much power you have to stop my mighty strength, I am the Devil of the Sea," Osinea said.

The Devil of the Sea suddenly sprayed the water onto Krome and Princess Adelia like a current of the big river but Krome and Adelia did not move or get wet as they both stood still in the middle of the air face to face with the Devil of the Sea.

"I see your powers are not bad at all . . . and take this!" the Devil of the Sea said.

Osinea flipped his tail to hit Krome and Adelia with the mighty power. They could feel the strong energies pass through their bodies as they both lost their strength and fell into the water. Krome reached out to pull Adelia's hand as he resumed his cosmic energy back and swam to the surface. Adelia almost passed out when Krome carried her out of the water. With help from Krome, she gained her energy back and they flew back into the air higher above the Devil of the Sea. They both stood in the middle of the air to absorb the energies from the lightning bolts with both of their arms up into the air; they transformed the lightning bolts into the light balls and projected the balls directly on top of the Devil of the Sea's head and body.

119

"Boom! Boom!" The explosions echoed across the sea. The strong explosive sounds were louder than the sounds of heavy bombs. The balls of the energies from the lightning bolts could only make the tiny scratches on the head of the Devil of the Sea as it were compared to the enormous size of his body. Osinea felt like someone had scratched his head; he did not get hurt at all. His body was like the rock of a big mountain when Krome and Adelia used the swords to kill him, even with all of their mighty strengths. The battle lasted for hours as Krome and Adelia tried their best. The battle caused more disasters and bad weather for the entire planet as the Devil of the Sea tried all his might to defeat Krome and Adelia. Rapidly he flew up from the water to gobble them with his most powerful suction and he swallowed them both into his stomach. The sea monster was very happy as he swam back to the bottom of the sea.

Princess Adelia was hurt very badly as she passed out inside the Devil of the Sea's belly. Krome was hurt too but he was still able to move around a little bit. Then he tried to sit down to meditate and concentrate to heal his body as well as to gain his energy back. Krome seemed to have a hard time to gain his energy back because everything inside the Devil of the Sea drained out the energies as Osinea's stomach tried to break down all the foods. Krome realized that he must help Princess Adelia to gain her energy back as soon as possible or she might be dead inside here. He moved to lift her body up to make her sit against his back so he could help her to absorb the energies into her body at the same time. For a while Krome was able to gain his cosmic energy slowly and he used that energy to bring Adelia's consciousness back. She was awakened after she received some of the energies from

Krome. Krome felt much better in both his strength and his mind and he started to talk to Princess Adelia.

"Adelia, how are you doing now? I'm glad that you've finally awakened," Krome said.

"Oh my head, what has happened, Krome?" Adelia asked.

"Well, we were swallowed by the Devil of the Sea and you got hurt and passed out. Now we are stuck inside his stomach," Krome said.

"How do we get out of here, Krome?" Adelia asked.

"I am thinking to find the way out," Krome said.

"First we must absorb our energies back, then we will find the way out," Krome continued.

"Adelia, you must concentrate in your meditation to heal yourself and to gain your cosmic energy . . . we must do that first," Krome told Adelia.

Then Adelia and Krome sat quietly inside the stomach of the Devil of the Sea to heal themselves and to absorb their cosmic energies. This would take longer than they thought because their energies were always fractionally pulled back by the Devil of the Sea. They spent many days to gain their full energies and completely healed their bodies inside the Devil of the Sea. Krome combined his energy with Princess Adelia to absorb not just their energies but the energies from the Devil of the Sea's body as well. Krome and Adelia were glowing inside the stomach of the Devil of the Sea as their bodies were full of the energies; the Devil of the Sea was weaker and weaker as he fell into his deep sleep. Princess Adelia and Krome used their cosmic energies to bust open the stomach of the God of the Sea but his stomach was stronger than they thought. The sea monster was uneasy as he felt the pain inside his stomach each time Krome and Adelia combined their energies to break his stomach. Krome

121

then remembered about Aquarus and he started to use his spiritual power to communicate with Aquarus to give him the advice of finding the way out.

"Hello, Krome, it looks like you both get stuck inside of the Devil of the Sea," Aquarus appeared inside Krome's head and spoke to him.

"Aquarus, what can we do to break free from inside of here?" Krome asked Aquarus.

"Krome, you and Adelia must absorb the entire energies of the sea monster and wait until the total solar eclipse occurs over his body then you and Adelia must combine your cosmic energies to kill him. Remember! You must wait until the right time. If you both miss it, you will be stuck in here until the next occurrence of the solar eclipse. This solar eclipse will occur in the next three days." Aquarus explained.

"Thank you, Aquarus, for your guidance," Krome and Adelia said.

"I will see you again Adelia and Krome," Aquarus said and disappeared.

Adelia and Krome sat back-to-back in their meditations and constantly absorbed the energies from the body of the sea monster as they had to wait until the sun totally eclipsed over the size of the moon on the body of the Devil of the Sea. The sea monster thought that they might be already dead inside his belly as he did not feel any kind of disturbance for almost two days. He felt so weak and he went back to sleep again. The Devil of the Sea slept like a dead monster because his energies were almost emptied by Adelia and Krome. They concentrated and were watching the sun and the moon with their spiritual insight powers as the planet was spinning days and nights; they kept counting the days and waited for the solar eclipse to happen.

11

Valimus's Conspiracy

In Almar Kingdom Diron and the other three wizards were so happy when they received the news that Krome and Princess Adelia were swallowed by the Devil of the Sea. Diron celebrated the victory of the sea monster with his fellow wizards and thanked the Devil of the Darkness. He informed Valimus about this good news, that they did not have to worry about Krome and Princess Adelia any more. Valimus began his conspiracy to kill all leaders who were loyal to King Hemiro by using his army's powers and Diron's wicked mind to turn and twist things around that those leaders would look like a group who plotted secret plans to overthrow the king. He forced some of the soldiers to say what he wanted them to say or their families and their lives would be executed. Before he began his evil work against those good leaders, Valimus had to wait for the right time. Princess Hollidia wanted to go to spend a week at the royal gardens and cabins about fifty miles from her father's palace and she had asked Lady Merida to come along with her. Valimus thought this would be the perfect time for him to execute his plan against the king so he sent Protus to escort Princess Hollidia and his mother to visit the royal cabins and gardens. After they left the palace, Valimus went to see the king and gave the king the information about who wanted to overthrow the king.

"Your Majesty, I . . . I would like to inform your majesty about the security and safety in our kingdom, especially concerning yourself, my king," Valimus spoke to the king.

"What do you mean the security and safety of our kingdom, Lord Valimus?" said King Hemiro. "Is it our neighborhood that wants to conquer our land?"

"Your majesty, this is not the people from outside; there are some leaders who have been keeping their eyes on your throne for some time but I have to gather all the proofs and would like to show your majesty," Valimus said and paused to see the king's reaction.

"I'm listening, please continue, Lord Valimus," the king said.

"With my intelligent groups and Diron's spiritual powers, we know that some of the leaders want to overthrow your majesty," Valimus told the king.

"How do you know for sure with this conspiracy, Lord Valimus?" the king said.

"Your majesty, during Princess Hollidia's trip to the Queen's tomb, we arrested two men from outside the kingdom and we know that they secretly work for some leaders in our kingdom. We tried to interrogate them for what purpose brought them to our kingdom but they refused to tell and would rather die," Valimus said.

"If so do you know who wants to overthrow my kingship?" the king said.

"Your majesty, if I tell you, your majesty will not believe me," Valimus answered.

"Go ahead Lord Valimus, I always trust you . . . I will continue to do so," the king said.

"Your majesty, it is about five people who are close to you including Prime Minister Deeconus and Lord Tamona. They secretly communicate with the people from Amoza Kingdom to overthrow your majesty and to destroy our kingdom. Your majesty must act quickly to remove these people before it is too late," Valimus advised the king.

"Your majesty, if you don't believe my words, I have the proof and witnesses to show you, your majesty," Valimus continued.

"Lord Valimus, you must show me at once," the king ordered.

"General Maxus, would you bring the witnesses and the criminals to show your majesty?" Valimus said.

General Maxus went outside the palace and ordered his soldiers to bring the two men, who were forced by Valimus to go along with his plan, to show to the king. Valimus had promised the two men not just to spare the lives of their families and their lives but would reward them with more gold, land, and power. King Hemiro believed Valimus as he slowly fell into Valimus's trap. He ordered Valimus to arrest all those leaders and put them in jail and then they would be brought to the king's court before they were thrown into the dungeon. Things were getting scary as Valimus and Diron gradually removed the people who would stand against them in the kingdom. Valimus felt like a king and he ordered his armies to look out around King Hemiro's palace because he pretended to protect the king. In fact he did not want the king to escape if he would find out. Valimus asked Diron to put a spell on the king so the king would become sick and then they both could use the drug to poison the king. Then Diron, the evil wizard, began to perform his black magic to put the king in a very painful experience and he would poison the king with his deadly drugs.

Now King Hemiro was in the real danger and no one could save him from this evil conspiracy. All the good leaders were arrested and imprisoned as Valimus completely gained the control over the kingdom. The king became very ill and he ordered Valimus to send the message to his daughter to come back to the palace as soon as possible. He wanted to see her and would have a few words with Merida and Protus in case something would happen to him.

"Lord Valimus you must send the guards to tell Protus and Princess Hollidia to come back to see me at once," the king ordered.

"Your majesty, I will send soldiers after them at once," said Valimus. "But you must take your medicine first your majesty, it will make you feel better, your highness."

Valimus told Diron to give medicine to make the king feel better so the king would not suspect him and Diron.

"Wizard Diron, please bring your best medicine for your king," Valimus said.

"Yes Lord Valimus, I will create the cure for the king with the best natural herbs and medicines that we have ever found," Diron replied.

"Your majesty, please you must take this medicine; it will make you feel better soon, my king," Diron said.

The King drank the medicine and after a while he felt much better as Diron had released his spell from his body.

"I feel a lot better and thank you, Wizard Diron," the king said.

"Lord Valimus, you don't need to send the guards to tell Princess Hollidia. . . . Now I feel much better already so just let them enjoy their stay at the royal resort," the king said.

"Your majesty, I am really happy to see you feel better," said Valimus. "I hope your majesty will soon gain your good health back, long live my king."

Diron finally prepared his last portion to kill the king when the time came. He was so excited that soon Princess Hollidia would fall into his arms and he would become the prince. He thought he would rule this kingdom with Valimus. Diron knew he would lose all his wizard powers when he touched the woman but with Princess Hollidia, he was willing to sacrifice his magic power with her beauty. He did not know who else had an eye on the princess and a heart for her.

"Lord Valimus, you are a real genius, the true king. I truly admire our great perception and vision . . . my future king," Diron said.

"You are the great wizard and my right-hand man. We will rule this kingdom together after my plan becomes a success," Valimus said.

"No one can ever stop me to become a king, no one. . . . Hah, hah, hah, hah," Valimus declared.

"Long live King Valimus . . . long live my future king," Diron made a compliment.

They both laughed and congratulated their victorious achievement as Valimus poured the wine into the glasses and invited Diron to join him with the joyful drink.

"I will have the biggest feast that you've ever seen when the time comes, I will definitely crown myself to be the king . . . the future king of Almar," Valimus said.

"Lady Merida will sit by my side and you . . . you will get your princess. Hah, hah, hah, hah. . . . I will rule this kingdom," Valimus continued and laughed.

"My precious Princess Hollidia, my beautiful angel . . . I will hold you dearly in my arms and love you until I die," Diron said.

Valimus knew for sure that Protus would not let Diron touch Princess Hollidia. He would use Diron to destroy Protus; thus, he did not have to worry about Protus's revenge for his father. If Diron and Protus would have the feud to possess Princess Hollidia, Valimus would announce the two to fight to the death and who won would take her. Valimus clearly comprehended Diron's wizard power and sword skill would dominate Protus's capability. This way he did not have to worry about Merida to say or to blame him as she would see for her own eyes that the two men fought over the woman as their destinations. Valimus now waited for Protus, Princess Hollidia, and Merida to come back from their vacation at the royal gardens and cabins then he would explain what had happened to the king and the other leaders who were arrested by him. He asked Diron to have the last portion ready for the king after Princess Hollidia had her last conversation with her father.

"Wizard Diron, you must finish your portion for the king and you will give this portion to the king after he has the last conversation with his daughter," Valimus said.

Diron looked at Valimus with his ugly smile and servant act, as he wanted to show his loyalty to his future king. He went to bring the small bottle of the deadly potion and kissed it before he handled it to Valimus.

"Your majesty . . . I want to practice these words with you because it will not be long, everyone in this kingdom will use these words to call you, Lord Valimus . . . I mean your majesty, King Valimus. . . . Heh, heh, heh," Diron said.

Valimus and Diron were excited as they waited for Protus, Merida, and Princess Hollidia to return and would finish their last act to take the king's life. Valimus explained to Diron that they had to make things smooth; therefore, no one would know their secret. Diron would put back his spell on the king and when the king became very sick, he would give the portion so the king would die as a natural cause. Diron told Valimus that his deadly potion was not detectable; a person would fall into sleep as the heart slowly stopped beating.

At the royal resort Princess Hollidia enjoyed her stay with Merida as they walked in the royal gardens filled with many species of colored flowers and plants. Merida's mind was still not sure what would be tomorrow as she thought about Valimus and Diron. She knew they were up to something behind the king and her. The only thing she could do was to keep praying to the God of the Enlightenment to protect her and her son, Protus, from the darkness and hoped some day she could reunite with her son, Krome, and Optimus in another world. She also was worried about Protus's future. What would happen to him when Valimus showed his true colors. Princess Hollidia seemed to recognize Merida's sadness and her cloudy mind but she was not sure what was bothering her. Her face was always hiding something back, even as she pretended to be happy. The princess walked side by side with Merida then she stopped over the stone bridge over the pond and looked at the fishes that were swimming in the water below, then she turned around to look at Merida.

"Lady Merida, isn't it beautiful in this royal garden? Look at the pretty colorful fishes swimming below, they look so happy," Princess Hollidia said.

"Yes it's sure; they are happy, your highness," Merida replied.

"And look over there . . . the purplish-white orchid flowers are so gorgeous among the red and pinkish ones," Princess Hollidia said and pointed at the flowers by the pond's side.

"I know that everything here is blooming and getting more beautiful," Merida said.

Princess Hollidia looked straight at Merida's eyes as she was quiet for a moment. She then tried to smile and continued her conversation as she walked off the bridge.

"Lady Merida, you seem to be sad. What is bothering you?" the princess asked.

"Why do you ask me this question, Princess Hollidia?" Merida said.

"Well . . . Well, you always look sad since the first day I saw you," Princess Hollidia explained to Merida.

Merida suddenly stopped walking and reached out to hold Princess Hollidia's hands as she started to tell the princess about her story.

"Perhaps you were too young to remember or maybe you have not understood what really happened to me about ten years ago," Merida told the princess.

"As I remember, I've heard that they had to bring you back here from Aquarium Mountain," Princess Hollidia recalled her memory.

"Yes, but what else did you know, your highness?" Merida asked.

Princess Hollidia put her hand on her mouth and rolled her eyes to look up as she tried to remember more things; she was quiet for a while because she could not remember any things else besides that.

"Well, that's all I know, Lady Merida," Princess Hollidia finally said to Merida.

"What happened besides they brought you back to the kingdom? Please, you can tell me, Lady Merida . . . we're just like one family," asked the princess.

"I see you did not know my story," Merida said.

"Please, would you mind telling me what exactly had happened at that valley?" the princess again asked.

"Well, this is a long story even before we escaped

from Almar," Merida began to tell her story to Princess Hollidia.

"Long before you were born, Optimus was a young handsome man who was the oldest son of Prime Minister Calibus, the previous prime minister of Almar. We were more than a friend as I grew up with him in the king's palace. I was in love with him since our teenage years; he treated me like his queen and we were undividable. Lord Valimus gained his fame on the battlefields through military and war experiences but back to that time he was Optimus's best friend. Valimus often asked and teased me as he always kept his eyes on me. He became the head of the general of Almar Armies after he won the war of defending the Almar Kingdom from the invasion of Amoza Empire. Since that day he had completely changed and planned to destroy Optimus as he pursued to have me. Optimus knew his secret plan and asked me to escape with him because he did not want to have a bloody feud with Valimus. Optimus did not care about the power and expected me to stay beside him. I never had the feeling for Valimus but he has a strong obsession with my charm even until today. Optimus and I, along with some other people, who did not like Valimus, escaped to the Aquarium Mountain region where nobody could follow or find us. After fourteen years, Optimus and I had two children and they both are boys, the older is Krome and the young one is Protus. We had lived very happily and peacefully in that hidden valley; we never thought to return as long as Valimus was still alive. But Valimus has never given up the search, with his power and Diron's wizard wisdom they finally found the place where we lived. Then they killed Optimus and blamed him that he betrayed King Hemiro. The soldier chased Krome to the cliff formation . . . he then fell of the cliff and died," Merida told

Princess Hollidia her story as the tears flooded out from her eyes.

Merida was sobered as she refreshed her painful memories in her mind. She was only strong by her belief in the God of the Enlightenment because without this belief she would perish. Princess Hollidia could not help herself from holding her tears as she heard Merida's sad story and knew that she had been suffering for too long. She held Merida's hands and tried to comfort her as she wanted to apologize such as to remind her to bring back this painful grief into her mind.

"I'm really sorry for what has happened to Krome and Optimus, Lady Merida," said Princess Hollidia. "I did not know until today. I'm so sorry to bring you into this saddest conversation. Sometimes life is not fair on this planet."

"No, it is not our fault, Princess, sometimes life has its own purpose," Merida said.

Merida and Princess Hollidia wiped their tears away from their faces as they saw Protus on his horse approach them from the distance.

"Please just keep this story to yourself for me, Princess Hollidia," Merida asked.

"Yes, Lady Merida, I promise . . . I will not tell the others," Princess Hollidia answered.

Protus jumped off from the horse and walked toward his mother and Princess Hollidia with his lovely smile as he greeted the princess and his mother.

"Good afternoon Princess Hollidia, good afternoon Mother, do you have a good time here? Everything is so beautiful here and the weather is much cooler than in the palace," Protus said.

"Good afternoon Protus," said Princess Hollidia. "Yes, it is very beautiful today; Lady Merida and I walked around to enjoy the sun and the abstract architectural design of the gardens with many kinds of plants, flowers, trees, and the ponds."

"Princess, you look well today. I seem to like this kind of weather here," said Protus. "I just want to check how Princess Hollidia and you are doing. I'm glad that both of you have a great time here. I will be around the resort to see what the guards are up to. I will see you later, Princess Hollidia."

"Yes, Protus, I will talk to you later," Princess said.

Protus did not want to disturb his mother and Princess Hollidia so he left them alone as he got back on his horse and rode away to see the guards on the other side of the resort.

12

Krome and Adelia Defeat the Devil of the Sea

The ocean was back to normal and the weather became clear with the blue sky over the sea water. Hundreds of miles away from the island and deepest into the shallow water Krome and Adelia had been sitting quietly for over three days inside the belly of the sea monster. Their bodies glowed like lightening bolts as they absorbed almost the entire energy from the monster's body. They looked through their spiritual visions carefully upon the sun and the moon above them. They waited for the solar eclipse to happen so they could use their combined powers to destroy the monster and to get out. Everything surrounding them was calm as the sun and the moon slowly moved close together. Aquarus again appeared in Krome's and Adelia's spiritual insight to remind them that the solar eclipse would happen in the next few hours.

"Hello Adelia, hello Krome . . . I see now your cosmic energies are fully loaded inside your bodies," said Aquarus. "Again you both must remember to combine your energies to float his body up to the surface when the solar eclipse completely occurs over the moon. Then you strike him when the sun emerges from the moon. . . . this is the only chance that you are able to defeat the Devil of the Sea."

"Yes Aquarus, we are ready and thank you for your guidance," Krome and Adelia said. "I will be with you until the moment it happens," said Aquarus. "I want to make sure you will not miss this one because the force of the darkness should not dominate the God of the Enlightenment. . . . May all the powers of the universe be with you."

"Again thank you, Aquarus for being here with us. Without you I don't know what to do and we would probably get stuck in here forever," Krome said.

The sea monster could hear the conversations between Aquarus, Adelia, and Krome but he could not do anything because his entire body was very weak. His cosmic energies were almost drained out from his body as Krome and Adelia were ready to strike him. He knew what would happen to him when the solar eclipse occured so he tried to communicate his spiritual power with the God of the Darkness. Now it was too late for him to concentrate to gain his power to be able to talk to the God of the Darkness. Without enough energies no one could hear his mind. He tried to withdraw the powers back from Krome and Adelia but it was impossible because his energy was almost nothing if it was compared to Krome and Adelia. He could not even move his body at all as he knew his life would soon come to the end. Aquarus sensed the sea monster's mind and he informed Adelia and Krome that they must keep concentrating and absorbing the energies from the sea monster; otherwise, they would lose their energies back to the Devil of the Sea.

"Krome, Adelia, you both must keep absorbing the energies and withholding these powers in your bodies until the time," Aquarus said.

"The sea monster now is trying to withdraw back the energies from the two of you; he has comprehended his danger is coming as the end of his life is near," Aquarus explained.

"Yes, Aquarus, we can feel his energies and his mind, which he is trying to channel with the God of the Darkness," Krome and Adelia said.

Now the moon slowly entered the straight point between the sun and the earth as the solar eclipse incompletely appeared in the sky above the sea monster. The bright blue sky was gradually turned to a shadow as the sun was blocked by the shape of the moon. Krome and Adelia combined their energies and transformed it into a spherical light. They both floated in the light ball as they used their energies to expand the size of the light ball inside the sea monster's belly. The radius of the light ball was expanding out, as the stomach of the Devil of the Sea was getting bigger and bigger. The sea monster had no energies left to defend him and his body started to float to the surface of the ocean. The size of the light ball expanded with the same rate of the solar eclipse as the body of the sea monster arose faster to the surface. The sun now was completely eclipsed and the sea monster floated on the sea water like a plastic ball. Krome and Adelia were waiting for the sun to completely emerge from the shape of the moon, then they would use all their cosmic energies to blast out the sea monster's body. As the moon totally moved out from the sun, the blasting sound shook the entire planet when Krome and Adelia used their combining cosmic energies to kill the sea monster. They finally defeated and destroyed the Devil of the Sea; they flew high into the air with their mighty powers. Their cosmic energies were many thousand times stronger than before after they both absorbed the entire energies from the sea monster.

Aquarus again appeared in Adelia's and Krome's insights to congratulate them for their victory over the sea monster.

"Congratulation to both of you . . . job well done. For you, Adelia . . . you have gained half of the extraordinary powers from the Devil of the Sea, that means, with this energies, you will be able to live for the next three thousand years," Aquarus said.

"And until then the fruits of the eternal life will be reproduced. . . . Krome you know what I'm talking about," Aquarus continued his conversation as he turned to tell Krome.

"Krome, your energy, when it is combined with Adelia's power, you both could destroy the entire planet," Aquarus informed Krome and Adelia as he tried to remind them. "You must remember to use your powers only with good intentions then at the end you both will become Holy Spirits. You both possess the God's will and powers . . . you must use your wisdom to protect the truth and the Enlightenment. Now it is the time you must save your mother and your brother from the forces of darkness . . . and may the power of the Enlightenment always be with both of you."

"Thank you, Aquarus for your advice . . . we will always remember your words and always serve the will of the God of the Enlightenment," Adelia and Krome responded.

"I will be with you whenever you need my help. I always keep my spiritual insight upon this planet and it is my responsibility. I will talk to both of you later," Aquarus said, then he disappeared from their insights.

Adelia and Krome looked like angels as their cosmic energies reached their maximum. They flew back to the island where they left the horse inside the cave. The horse was safe and the entire island was not much damaged from the disasters. They brought the horse back to the beach of the island and tried to communicate with the great white whales. They thanked the whales for their help and told them that they could go back to their place. Krome and Adelia were able to use the horse to fly across the ocean because their energies were superb after they defeated the sea monster. They both could sense the danger of Merida and Protus as well as King Hemiro and Princess Hollidia.

"Krome, we're better to get to Almar Kingdom sooner because I'm able to see Diron's and Valimus's plan as they want to kill the king," Adelia said.

"Yes I feel the same way, Adelia," said Krome. "We will ride this horse across the ocean to Almar shore."

Krome asked Adelia to get on the horse first and he rode behind her. They rode on the horse fast along the beach and then took off into the air away from the island. They flew over the clouds toward the Almar Kingdom and after only a day they arrived and landed on the Almar shore.

13

Krome Reunited with His Mother and Protus

Krome and Adelia rode on the horse and flew over the mountains and jungles direct to the royal resort where Merida, Protus, and Princess Hollidia stayed. They landed the horse on the road not far from the royal resort and rode very fast. As they got closer to the gate of the resort, the guards on the post spotted them from a distance and they informed Protus about the strangers. Protus ordered the guards to take precautions and he asked more soldiers to ride the horses along with him toward Krome and Adelia. He came face to face with Krome and Princess Adelia; he tried to stop them from entering into the resort.

"Stop . . . who are you? Where are you from, strangers?" Protus asked.

"Protus, my name is Krome and she is Princess Adelia." Krome introduced himself and Princess Adelia to his brother.

"How do you know my name? We have never met and what business brings you both to our kingdom?" Protus said, while he looked straight to Princess Adelia. He was amazed with her absolutely beautiful appearance as he thought that he had never met the prettiest woman like her in his entire life. He rode his horse closer to them and he was attracted to Princess Adelia suddenly.

"Protus, Krome is your older brother and I'm his partner," Adelia told Protus.

"No, you don't have to trick me. I never had a brother," Protus denied.

"Yes, I'm your brother, Protus . . . your mind is drugged by Valimus and Diron, that is why you cannot remember your past," Krome explained to his brother.

Protus still did not believe Krome and Adelia because he had completely lost his mind with the drug from Diron. He wanted to challenge and to kill Krome as he wanted to capture Princess Adelia. He asked Krome and Adelia to get off from the horse and ordered his soldiers to surround them. Krome and Adelia got down from the back of the horse and they knew that Protus wanted to arrest them. Krome told Adelia the only way to save Protus to remember his past was to hit him so the drug inside his body would be pushed out from his blood and then he would heal his brother with his power.

Protus quickly jumped off his horse and walked close to Krome as he was looking at his brother from head to toe. He asked them to surrender themselves to him and if Krome refused, he would challenge him to death. Protus looked at the Aquarus's sword next to Krome's waist as he spoke to his brother.

"You must surrender yourself to us; otherwise, you will fight to death with me and my armies before we let you go free," Protus said.

Krome had agreed to challenge his brother. He drew Aquarus's sword and threw it on the ground. He told Protus that he did not need to use the sword, only with his two bare hands. He also asked Protus to use Aquarus's sword if he wanted to. Protus walked toward Aquarus's

140

sword and he tried to pick it up but he could not even lift it a little bit from the ground. He was so mad and turned around to look at Krome as he drew the sword from his horseback. He swung and slashed the blade at his brother but Krome moved like the speed of the wind and the shadow. Protus tried very hard to cut Krome with his blade and he realized that it was impossible for him to defeat a warrior like Krome. Protus then ordered his guards to join him to kill Krome; they surrounded him with the spears and swords. As the guards ran in to stab and slash the blades at Krome, he flew up and spun his body into the air with a single strike. The soldiers and Protus dropped all their swords and spears as they fell down to the ground. More soldiers from the resort had come out to help Protus; thus, they ended up like the rest. Merida and Princess Hollidia had heard the incident outside the resort so they both came out to see what was really happening. Protus was hurt as he coughed out with blood; he looked up at Krome and asked him.

"Who are you? Why do you possess so much power?" Protus said.

"I'm your brother and my name is Krome. . . Can you remember now?" Krome said.

Krome reached his hand to touch his brother, trying to heal his wound but Protus moved away with panic because he thought Krome would hurt him more. Krome told his brother that he tried to heal his body. Princess Adelia stood nearby and watched without interfering between Krome and Protus; she knew exactly what Krome tried to do to help his brother to bring back his memories.

"Please don't move and don't be afraid, I just want to heal your wound. If I want to kill you and even if you have wings, you won't be able to escape," Krome told his brother.

141

Krome used his cosmic energy to push out the drug from Protus's body and to heal him at the same time. Protus felt Krome's energy pass through his body and suddenly he felt well and stronger than he used to be. He got up and thanked his brother for the power of healing and he began to apologize for his discourteous act earlier.

"Thank you, Krome, for the healing and please accept my apology for my rudeness. You are the greatest warrior who is able to defeat my sword skill for the first time with your bare hands . . . you defeat not just me but all my men too," Protus said.

"You're very welcome, Protus, I have no intention to hurt you but I have to make you wounded so I could push the drug out from your body and you will be able to remember your past. Now you can think back to all your past without harming yourself. Valimus and Diron used the drug to make you forget all of your past because they don't want you to avenge our father. They are the force of darkness; they are the ones who will be responsible for their sins and criminal acts against our family," Krome explained to Protus.

Princess Hollidia and Merida arrived at the scene wondering what was going on a while ago as they saw all the soldiers were still moving on the ground after they got the hits from Krome. They looked at Princess Adelia and Krome as they turned to ask Protus about what had happened and why all these guards were hurt on the ground.

"Protus, what has happened to all these guards?" Merida asked as she turned to look at Krome with a strange feeling just like she knew him before.

"We are trying to arrest these people but we are defeated by him," said Protus. "They came from far away to save us from the force of darkness."

Merida looked at Krome again as she wondered if she

had met him somewhere before. She could not recognize her son because he had changed so much after he ate Oradius's fruits. She turned around to look at Princess Adelia and admired in her mind how beautiful Adelia was. She thought these two persons resembled angel appearances. Princess Hollidia was speechless when she saw Krome and Adelia. She also thought that she had never seen persons who looked so perfect with gorgeous physical grace and attraction, but she wondered why Protus tried to hurt people like this; they appeared to be the good, friendly people with no harm.

"Who are you, the great warriors?" Merida asked Krome and Adelia.

"My name is Krome and she is Princess Adelia. . . . I'm your older son, Mother," Krome said to his mother with a gentle smile.

"Krome. . . . it could not be, oh my God . . . are you really my son?" Merida said.

"Yes, Mother, I fell from the tree into the cliff when I was chased by Valimus's knight near Freewill Valley but I was saved by the giant golden eagle in the midst of the fall."

Krome explained to his mother as he pulled down his short leather jacket to show her the family's mark on his right shoulder.

"Here is my family's mark, Mother, I'm really Krome," Krome said.

Merida was quiet for a moment as she looked at the mark on Krome's shoulder. She put her left hand to cover her mouth and started to cry with joy as she fell down on her knees. She was about to faint with this greatest news. Adelia quickly moved to hold her as Krome walked close to his mother. He held her hands up and looked at her face. Merida embraced her son with tears of joy; thus, she felt like she had been reborn.

"Krome . . . Krome . . . my beloved son, I thought I had lost you all these years. . . . Thank God for saving you," said Merida. "I thought I would never see you again in this life."

Krome hugged his mother and he tried to comfort her as Princess Adelia still kneeled down on her knees next to him. Adelia was very excited to see the family reunion and she was very happy for Krome as well as for herself. Krome lifted his mother up and held her close to his heart as he spoke to her.

"Mother, from now on nobody can hurt you any more, you will have your happiness back and will live in peace," said Krome. "We are no longer the victims."

Protus started to see his memories come back as he recalled his past. He remembered when he used to play with Krome and saw what had happened at Freewill. He remembered that day Valimus rode the horse and swung the sword at his father. He was holding on to his mother's legs while they pulled her away from him and he even still remembered his words, "Please don't hurt my Mother." He began to hate Valimus and Diron as he remembered everything in the past. He walked close to his brother and he again apologized to Krome.

"Krome, my great brother, I'm very sorry for my rudeness and I'm very happy for this moment as our family finally came together," Protus said.

Krome turned around to give Protus a hug and he spoke to congratulate his brother for getting his memories back. Protus embraced his brother with eyes full of tears and joyfulness. Merida could not imagine that she could live to see this day as she saw her two sons embrace each other. She was very glad to see Protus get his memories back.

"I'm very happy for you, Protus . . . you have your memories back," said Krome.

Krome turned to look at Princess Hollidia and talked to her as she kept her eyes on him.

"You must be Princess Hollidia, I'm pleased to meet you, your highness and I'm sorry for not introducing myself first because with all these excitements," Krome said.

"Yes, Krome, my name is Hollidia and I'm a daughter of King Hemiro. It is my greatest pleasure to meet you. I'm very happy to see you have finally reunited with your family and my father will be very pleased to see you," Princess Hollidia said.

Princess Hollidia's heart filled with joy as she felt like she finally had met her prince. She looked at Krome with her lovely smile and her eyes always glanced at him. She felt that she wanted to hold him or be held by him. This was the first time that she was really falling in love with a man at first sight. The temperature in her body seemed to keep changing as her mind fell deeper into this feeling. She held it back when she saw Princess Adelia. She knew that Krome already had someone by his side. She realized that they were a matching pair and their charms were equal. Her conscience told her to stop this feeling because it would be impolite and it was sinful to steal the lover from someone's heart. Protus withdrew his feeling completely from Princess Adelia when he knew Krome was his brother and Princess Adelia was with his brother. He looked at Princess Hollidia as she turned to look at him. He gave the princess his courageous smile and she smiled back at him. They both realized perhaps this was the path that brought them together in this life. She walked close to Protus and reached out to hold his hands and this was the first time that she held the man's hands and accepted him as her man.

"Protus, I'm happy that you got your memories back and reunited with your brother, Krome," Princess Hollidia said.

"Thank you, your highness," Protus said.

Princess Hollidia lifted her left hand and put her fingers slightly over Protus's lips and she gently spoke to him.

"Please just call me, Hollidia. . . . Protus, you have a great brother," the princess said.

Protus felt his body warm as Princess Hollidia held his hands tighter and he looked into her eyes, he knew she opened her heart to him for the first time and she felt the same way. He lifted his right arm to hold her shoulder and pulled her close to him.

Krome again introduced Princess Adelia to his mother and explained to her how he came to meet Adelia. He was happy to see everyone was very joyful and especially for his mother. He then explained to Princess Hollidia about Valimus's and Diron's conspiracy and plan to kill her father.

"Princess Hollidia, you must know that your father is in danger because Valimus plans to crown himself to be the king. He will kill your father by letting Diron use his poisonous potion when the time comes. This will happen in the next two days after you have returned to your palace. Valimus has used Diron to put the spell on your father to make him become very ill and then he will use his potion to poison the king," Krome explained.

"If Valimus succeeds, he will reward Diron with Princess Hollidia," said Krome "and Valimus will force my mother to marry him."

146

"What can we do to stop this conspiracy? I think we need your help," Hollidia asked.

"We play along with his game," said Krome, "but first I will train Princess Hollidia and Protus to gain their strength and to use their energy to be able to defeat Diron's capability and Valimus's strong knights. This will not take long to become well-trained warriors. Adelia, please could you keep my mother company while I'm doing this?"

"Yes, Krome, it is my great pleasure to talk to your mother," Adelia said as she walked with Merida back to the royal resort.

Krome used his powers to heal all the guards and asked them to go back to the resort and said no one could leave the Almar Palace. Krome first asked Protus and Princess Hollidia to sit back-to-back with him facing out in three directions and they must use their minds to concentrate in their meditation to absorb the energies surrounding them. Not for long Princess Hollidia and Protus had channeled their energies and they absorbed it to gain their strength. After this process was completed, they used the swords to practice their moves and jumped into the air floating their bodies like the butterflies. Krome trained them to use their energies to lift their bodies and to swim through the air. Protus and Princess Hollidia were easily adapted to this environment as they were practicing to master their skills. Krome first used his cosmic energy to help them as he had used it to train Princess Adelia.

Now Protus and Princess Hollidia were able to use their energies to fly into the air higher and their sword skills were improved faster than they could think as their strengths were grown in their bodies. They were amazed with Krome's powers, which could help them to train their bodies, and to become the greater warriors in a very short time.

Princess Adelia sat and had conversations with Merida in the royal gardens. She told Merida her story and how she decided to follow Krome's footstep.

"I was chosen and sent to be eaten by the giant snake named Serpenum and known as the God of the Snake, just to save the people in my kingdom. Every hundred years the snake came up from the bottom of the great lake to eat the virgin princess," Adelia said.

"Yes, I have heard the legend of this snake when I was a child," Merida said.

"I was saved by Krome as he showed up and killed the snake," Adelia continued.

"When Krome brought me back to my kingdom, the evil wizard who served in my father's kingdom as the highest wizard, put curses on the people and blamed me and Krome with the death of the snake. That is why God became mad and cursed the whole kingdom. . . . My father was tricked by the wizard and he allowed the wizard to use his people to kill Krome and me . . . but Krome again had saved me from Mongon, the evil wizard and the force of darkness," Adelia told Merida as she sat close to her.

Merida gently touched Adelia's hair as she looked at Adelia's beautiful face while she listened to Adelia's story. She was very happy that Krome had found the most beautiful princess in the whole planet to come along with him. She now was the happiest person on the planet after she reunited with her son. She knew Krome possessed the highest power that could cure the sickness and not just that, he also brought along the sweetest young woman with him. She really loved Adelia like her own daughter and she remembered when she decided to escape with Optimus from Valimus's wicked plan. She kissed Adelia's head as she tried to comfort her painful past.

"God has blessed your soul as he has done for Krome . . . you are the perfect pair and no one could ever break you both apart," Merida said.

"Then we traveled across the ocean to here but in the middle of the ocean we were attacked by the sea monster, known as the Devil of the Sea, and we were swallowed by him. We were stuck inside of him for more than three days and with the help from Aquarus's Holy Spirit, we were able to defeat the sea monster after the moment of the solar eclipse a day before we arrived here," Adelia told Merida.

"We heard the sound of the explosion that shook the entire planet. We did not know what happened and we thought maybe a comet collided on the surface of the planet somewhere," Merida replied.

"The sound came from the explosion of the sea monster's body," Adelia said.

"See, God always protects both of you . . . you are both the will of God. Adelia, I feel very peaceful when I'm close to you. Somehow I feel as you are my own child . . . you're precious to me and my son and welcome to our family," Merida said.

"Lady Merida, you have the greatest son in the entire planet," Adelia said.

Krome was glad to see his brother and Princess Hollidia mastered their skills so fast after he helped them unlock their potential energies. Now Protus and Princess Hollidia challenged each other with the swords; Protus was truly amazed with her capability of defend herself as he knew she had never held the sword in her entire life. He could not even defeat her because she now possessed the power and the skill which were equal to his. Their bodies looked stronger and more charming than they used to look after their energies developed in their bodies. They both walked to Krome and showed their gratitude.

"Krome thank you, I have never realized that these energies exist around us," Protus spoke to Krome, "but without your powers, we would never have learned to become like this."

"I truly appreciate your guidance, Krome . . . I never thought that I could do this thing," said Princess Hollidia. "You have put magic inside my body."

"Now you have learned the power of the God of the Enlightenment and you only use it for good purposes. The more you practice and use it you will learn and improve to the higher level both for your skills, energies, and intellectual. I think that you are ready to face Diron and Valimus and we should get ready to go back to the king's palace. We need to tell Mother and Adelia in the royal gardens," Krome said.

They both walked into the resort toward Merida and Adelia and the guards respected them as their king. Adelia stood up as they approached and Merida got up to look at her sons again. She put her hands on Krome's and Protus's faces and smiled as she spoke to both of them.

"After all these years, the two brothers have reunited and you both have found your princesses. And I'm the happiest person on the entire planet," Merida said.

"What should we do next Krome?" Princess Hollidia asked.

"First you all must act normal; Adelia and I will not show up with you. I want Princess Hollidia to find out herself but Adelia and I will sneak into King Hemiro's room without letting anyone know because we want to protect the king. Princess Hollidia you must act as usual and pretend to cry when you hear Diron and Valimus announced the king's death. Mother . . . you will act the same and you will go along with Princess Hollidia. Protus, you must tell your guards not to talk or leak out any information to Valimus and Diron and for Protus . . . you will go with Princess Hollidia and Mother," Krome explained.

"For all of you, the guards, I ask you to stay out and not to inform any of Valimus's men; otherwise, you will end up hurting yourself," Krome warned the guards.

Protus rode on his horse leading the group back to the king's palace as Merida and Princess Hollidia rode in the wagon behind him followed by the guards. Krome and Adelia rode on the horse behind them as he used his spiritual power to focus into the king's palace. Halfway to the palace Krome told Protus that he and Adelia needed to go into the king's room first. They flew from the back of the horse up higher into the air and Krome reminded his brother to remember the secret plan he should do when he got back to the king's castle and Protus should remind all of his guards to do the same thing.

"Remember Protus . . . I will see you there . . . remind all your guards to keep it low when they are back at the palace," Krome said as he flew away toward Almar Palace.

Krome and Adelia concealed themselves with their magical powers to become invisible as they flew and landed into King Hemiro's room. The king was sleeping and he was still sick under Diron's magical spell. Krome and Adelia walked quietly toward the king's bed as Krome tried to wake the king up. The king opened his eyes and he was scared to see Krome and Adelia by his bed. He almost called the guards but Krome used his power to hold the motion and explained to him about Valimus's conspiracy.

"Your majesty, my name is Krome and she is Princess Adelia, we come here to rescue you from Valimus's secret plan. He wants to kill you and take over your kingdom. Now you are under Diron's spell, that is why you have became very ill. Valimus has ordered Diron to make a poisonous potion to kill you tomorrow. I will use my power to heal you from this evil spell and you must promise me not to let anyone know about this," Krome explained to King Hemiro. King Hemiro agreed with Krome and let him heal his body. Krome sent his spiritual power into the king's body to chase the evil power out of him. The king suddenly felt well as he had never been sick and he started to believe Krome.

"Great Warrior, thank you for saving my life and my kingdom; I don't know how I could ever pay you back," the king said.

"Your majesty, we do not want anything from you and we are here just to protect good people like you from the force of darkness. . . . We have met your daughter, Princess Hollidia, at the royal resort and we have explained to her as well as my mother and my brother, Merida and Protus, about this situation. They will pretend that they have not known about this conspiracy. We want to see how far Valimus and Diron will go with their plan," Krome said to the king.

"You are Krome . . . you are the oldest son of Lady Merida and you are my long lost nephew. I know Lady Merida always thinks of you as she thought you fell and died in the river at Aquarium Mountain. God has blessed your life," King Hemiro said.

"You must pretend you are getting sick and when Diron gives you the potion, I will use my magic power to switch with this one. You can drink water from this one and you must pretend that you have died. You will see what will really happen. Adelia and I will be in here invisible, as we want to see how Valimus is playing his game," Krome said.

King Hemiro was very happy to see Krome and Adelia to rescue him and his kingdom. He stood up to hug Krome and Adelia and thank them for their great help.

"Thank you again Krome and Princess Adelia, without you, my life would end tomorrow. This must be the God's will to save my life and my kingdom," said King Hemiro. "I will be ready to see Valimus's and Diron's faces for the last time."

King Hemiro called his royal servants in as he lay down on his bed pretending he was very ill. He ordered the guard to go to inform Valimus and Diron that his condition was getting worse but Valimus told Diron to ignore the king because he thought the king's life would be ended as soon as Princess Hollidia had returned. King Hemiro was very upset and disappointed with them after all these years he had trusted them the most with all his heart. Krome told the king to calm down and tried to be ready for the final show down.

14

Defeats of Valimus and Diron

Princess Hollidia, Protus, and Merida had arrived in front of the palace as Valimus and Diron with other of their men walked to welcome the princess back from her vacation. Protus got down from his horse and bowed to Valimus and Diron as he used to do and he informed them Princess Hollidia and Merida had returned.

"Good afternoon Lord Valimus . . . Good afternoon Wizard Diron. Princess Hollidia has returned, my lord," Protus said.

"Well done Protus . . . Did Princess Hollidia and Lady Merida have a good time? Perhaps next time I will join and spend time with them at the royal resort," Valimus said.

"Yes my lord . . . you should, it was beautiful at the resort, my lord," Protus said.

Protus went to open the wagon's door for the princess and his mother to get out and he looked at Princess Hollidia as he bowed to her as usual. He held the princess's hand as she stepped down from the royal wagon.

"Thank you Protus . . . I really enjoyed the trip and maybe next time we can stay longer at the resort," Princess Hollidia said as she stood looking around in front of the castle as she had missed to see some of the leaders who used to come to greet her and especially her father.

154

Protus held his mother's hand and helped her to get down from the wagon while Princess Hollidia questioned Valimus about the absence of her father and other leaders.

"Lord Valimus, where are my father and the other leaders?" Princess Hollidia asked.

"Your highness, the king is very ill. . . . Diron has been trying everything to cure the king but his majesty is still not getting better . . . and the other leaders . . . the other leaders, you will find out when you see the king . . . ," Valimus answered the princess, then he took a deep breath as he pretended to show his remorse.

Princess Hollidia rapidly acted in panic as she pretended to show how worried she was with the great concern about her father. Diron looked at the princess's face as he felt burning inside to share his love with her. He was really in love with her and he recognized she was getting more beautiful than ever. He tried to comfort the princess as he saw her commotion.

"Your highness . . . I'm truly sorry for my incapability to cure and save your father. Sometimes life has its own destiny . . . you must be strong, your highness," said Diron "I have been trying all my best to save the king. . . . I have combined every herb to make a last medicine for the king but the medicine may be too strong for the king if he has the reaction, it can kill him." Valimus thought Diron was out smarting the princess and everyone. He knew this was a killing potion which he would give to the king soon if the king died, it was reasonable to explain. Valimus was even more surprised to hear these words, which came out from Diron's mouth as he thought this was the perfect plan and he even admired Diron more.

Princess Hollidia hurried to get inside the palace to see her father as Merida and the rest of the people followed her to the king's room. She ran to his bed and sat beside holding his hands as she and the king made the eye's signal; she cried and held onto him.

"Father . . . Father, please you must get better . . . you cannot die on me because I want you to live to see your grandchildren . . . please you must live," Princess Hollidia said as her tears flowed down from her eyes. The king acted as if he was in serious condition, called his daughter's name a few times and coughed up before he spoke to her.

"Hollidia . . . my beloved daughter . . . I . . . I think I may not live longer to see your children and I don't want to die . . . my beautiful princess . . . please look at me, I want to see your face for the last time," said the king. "You are getting more pretty than ever. Lady Merida, please come closer, I want you to take care of Princess Hollidia for me . . . and Protus . . . you must promise me to take good care of Princess Hollidia. . . . Your great-grandfather was a good king before my father and me . . . I want . . . I want to crown you as the next king of Almar Kingdom . . . will you promise me to be a good king?"

"Your majesty, I promise your highness that I will be a good king and take good care of Princess Hollidia until the day I die," Protus said to the king as he kneeled down by the side of King Hemiro's bed.

Valimus silently laughed inside his mind as he thought it was too easy for Protus to be the king. Diron was very mad inside when he heard the king's proposal to crown Protus to be king and look after Princess Hollidia. He now wanted to kill the king right away as badly as he wanted to destroy Protus but he understood he must stay cool. Valimus went outside the king's room and ordered his men to be ready as he knew the final showdown would

156

happen soon. Diron excused the king to go to his room to get the potion and he walked faster to his castle. He went into his wizard room and closed the door behind him. He started his strongest spell on the king and took the potion back to the king's room. Krome used his spiritual power to speak to King Hemiro's mind that he must act as he had the worst pain inside his body because he could feel Diron's evil force enter the king's room. Krome defeated the force of darkness just like a person blew out the light of a candle. King Hemiro asked for Diron to give him more medicine as he pretended he was very painful inside his body.

"Wizard Diron, please hurry, you must give me more medicine for my pain. . . . I think I will die with this pain," said the king as he blinked one of his eyes at Princess Hollidia. "My beloved daughter . . . I don't want to die . . . please someone help me."

Princess Hollidia and Merida cried as they pretended that they were very worried about the king's health. Diron walked by Valimus outside the king's room and he talked very quiet at Valimus's ear to inform him about the strongest spell which he had used on the king. He showed Valimus the potion before he walked into the king's room. Valimus followed Diron as he entered through the door of the king's room. Diron hurriedly gave Princess Hollidia the potion and told her to give it to the king. She put the potion on the small table next to the king's bed as she tried to lift her father to a sitting position. Krome quickly used his magic power to switch the little vase of the potion and told Princess Hollidia's mind that he just switched the vase so she could go ahead to give it to her father. She took the potion in the vase and helped the king to drink from it.

"Here Father, please you must drink this medicine, it

will make you feel better soon . . . please don't die . . . you must live, Father," Princess Hollidia said.

King Hemiro drank the potion all from the little vase and a moment later he pretended as he had passed away. Princess Hollidia cried out loud with her tears as she regretted that the king finally lost his life.

"Father . . . Father . . . oh God please have mercy on my father's soul. . . . Lady Merida, my beloved father has passed away," Princess Hollidia said as she cried and held on to her father's body. Merida kneeled by her side next to the king as she mourned for the loss of the king. Protus also kneeled next to the king and mourned along with his mother and Princess Hollidia. Valimus spoke to Merida and Princess Hollidia that he was greatly sad and wanted to share their sorrow for the loss of the king.

"Princess Hollidia, I'm very sad that the king lost his life . . . you don't have to worry because Diron and I will take a good care of you. . . . For Protus to become a king we will think it over later but for now I will be in charge for the king," Valimus said.

"And you must marry Diron because he has saved your life from the mysterious illness . . . don't you remember? Without his wizard power, you would have died a long time ago. You must know he is very loyal to you and your father," Valimus said.

"Lord Valimus, I cannot let you do that to Princess Hollidia," Protus said.

"Protus, if you want to live, you must do what I say," Valimus said out loud to Protus.

"No my lord, I will not let you do this because I'm the new king and you must listen to me. Didn't you see what King Hemiro just said before he passed away?" Protus spoke clearly as he looked at Valimus's eyes.

"I don't care what he said because I'm the new king

now. You must look around you, all these guards will listen to me. And besides, if you want Princess Hollidia, you must ask Wizard Diron. Does he allow you to have her? If not, you must defeat him before you can take her," Valimus said.

"Lady Merida, you must prepare to marry me in the next few days," Valimus said.

Protus accepted the challenge with Diron to fight to the death for Princess Hollidia as he went outside in front of the king's palace with Diron and Valimus. The guards followed them to the court in the garden in front of the castle. Only Princess Hollidia and Merida were inside the king's room with Krome, Adelia, and the king. Hemiro opened his eyes and got up; he could not believe Valimus and Diron would do this to him. He looked from the window down to the court and asked Krome if Protus alone could defeat Diron, Valimus, and the rest of his men.

"Krome, do you think Protus can handle these people by himself?" King Hemiro asked.

"Your majesty, I've trained Protus with Princess Hollidia to master their sword skills and to control their potential energies. I believe Protus can defeat Diron, Valimus, and his men without any help from us," Krome said.

Princess Hollidia told her father that she would go down to help Protus. The king was really surprised and worried for her safety because he had never seen his daughter hold any sword for her entire life.

"My beloved child, how can you help because you cannot even defend yourself?" the king said.

"Father . . . I'm no longer the victim. Krome has trained me to be a great warrior and I will prove it to you . . . you will see, Father," Princess Hollidia said.

Princess Hollidia picked up the royal sword and went

159

outside the king's palace; she walked toward the royal court to joint Protus. Valimus and Diron laughed at the princess as she walked through the guards to join Protus in the middle of the court.

"Well . . . Well, Princess Hollidia, what are you doing here? Well, it looks like you want to save your future king," Valimus said to Princess Hollidia.

"Even if you kill Protus, I will not let you decide who I should marry. If Diron wants me, he has to defeat me first," Princess Hollidia said.

Diron laughed and looked at the princess with his ugly smile as he asked one of his guards to bring the sword for him. He walked close to Princess Hollidia and looked straight into her eyes as he spoke to her with his contempt.

"I respect you as my future princess, my beloved wife, but if you choose to fight against me, I will be glad to show you my power and teach you the lesson so you will respect your future husband for life," Diron said.

"And which one of you wants to test my power first?" Diron said.

"Princess Hollidia, you must be careful, please don't underestimate his power and let me be the one . . . who will teach him how to respect the woman," Protus said.

Protus walked to Diron and told him that he would challenge him first. Diron secretly used his dark power to throw the energy ball toward Protus's chest but Protus moved like the wind as he floated his body into the air and hit Diron's dark energy ball down to the ground and he softly landed on the top of it. Diron and Valimus were very surprised to see how Protus could know this skill of the potential energies. Diron again repeatedly projected the stronger energy balls toward Protus and Krome quickly sent his spiritual power to explain to Protus and

Princess Hollidia just to relax when Diron's energy hit them, they must float along and absorb that energy into their bodies. They then could transform that dark energy into their own and they could use that energy to fire back to Diron. Protus followed every word from Krome as he softly floated in the air and absorbed Diron's dark energies. He landed gently on the ground farther from Diron and then like the speed of a lightning bolt, he fired back the energy ball at Diron with the speed of light. Diron was hit harder as he felt the energy pass through his body but he used his wizard power and quickly recovered his strength. He was even more surprised with Protus's capability as he felt he could lose in this battle. Valimus knew that he had to use his men to distract Protus's mind and let Diron do his work to defeat him. Valimus ordered six of his strongest knights to help Diron so they could defeat Protus. Princess Hollidia flipped her body higher into the air and landed next to Protus and told him to concentrate on the fight with Diron and the rest of the knights he must leave to her. Valimus, Diron, and their men were completely speechless as they saw Princess Hollidia fly higher into the air with the sword in her hand like a bird.

"What is the matter Diron? Can you feel the heat now?" Princess Hollidia asked.

"Don't be foolish Princess Hollidia. If you don't want to get hurt you must stay out from this fight," Diron warned Princess Hollidia.

Valimus sent another six of his men in as he saw the situation may be worse, the way he saw Princess Hollidia's movement was not so simple. He thought she might be another Protus in this battle. He ordered his soldiers to attack Protus and Princess Hollidia without mercy as he wanted to kill both of them.

"You must defeat them; if not, you may all die with us," Valimus said.

Valimus's knights fought like the bulls as they slashed the blades at Princess Hollidia and Protus. Princess Hollidia fought like an angel as her body moved with the speed of the wind, flipping and floating in the air and brought down Valimus's knights one by one. King Hemiro was watching his daughter's motions without a blink of his eye as he could never dream that his beautiful daughter could accomplish the skills beyond the great warrior. He wanted to come down to see the fight closer but Krome told the king to wait for the right moment. Valimus kept sending more of his men to fight against Protus and Princess Hollidia and he used his potential energy to fire the ball at Protus from behind. Princess Hollidia saw that then she used the skill which Krome just showed to Protus to absorb the dark energy ball from Valimus as she flew up higher into the air. She spun her body down like a spiral string and with a single strike all of Valimus's knights fell down to the ground with hard hits and were badly wounded as they lay down in the circle. Princess Hollidia landed gently on the ground as she sat down like the statue of the Buddha. She put down her royal sword on the ground and tried to absorb the energies surrounding her as she was sitting still on the ground in the middle of the court. Valimus saw Princess Hollidia sit down with her eyes closed; he projected a stronger energy ball at her. With both of her eyes closed, she was able to sense all energies moving around her body including Valimus's dark energy which he was throwing at her. Princess Hollidia was spinning her body back into the air like the sorcerer as she lifted both of her hands projecting directly toward Valimus's dark energy.

Princess Hollidia was able to absorb Valimus's energy ball from a distance and she was able to maintain her body in the middle of the air spontaneously. She reversed his energy and threw it back to him but Valimus jumped into the air as fast as he could escape from getting hit. Valimus thought he was right about Princess Hollidia's capability. He drew his sword and flew closer to her and he attacked her constantly but the princess moved and protected her body from his merciless blade faster than Valimus could imagine. With the great training of the fighting skill and energetically dominating technique from Krome, Princess Hollidia could unlock the mysterious key of the physically potential energy and absorb or dispense it very precisely. She even made things move by using her mind with spiritual power as she was capable to move her royal sword from the ground onto her left hand in the middle of the air. Valimus was very impressed by her power and he had no idea where she had learned all these magical motions and skills. Princess Hollidia comprehended the power Krome showed her was not limited, it would grow and improve as long as the person kept learning, practicing, and using it. She realized this was the power of the God of the Enlightenment, which always existed throughout the universe for the good people to use it against the force of darkness. Valimus again took charge as he was spinning his body like the arrow through the air direct to Princess Hollidia and fiercely slashed his blade on her. She blocked every move of his blade without opening her eyes and the sparks of light appeared each time the two blades collided together in the air. She grew stronger as the battle went on. Valimus was interested and more surprised as he had never fought with the greatest warrior like her. He seemed to get weaker as he kept using his dark energy to attack Princess Hollidia because men sometimes under-estimate the woman's strength.

King Hemiro was amazed to see how his daughter could ever stand boldly face to face in the battle with a great warrior like Valimus. He had gained the confidence and comfort in his daughter's competency as the battle went on between her and Valimus. The king was very grateful with Krome's mighty rescue that he had not just saved his life and his kingdom but he had transformed Princess Hollidia into the greatest woman warrior who he had ever seen in his whole life. He felt like he wanted to hold her in his arms and kiss her head like a loving father used to do to his child.

"Krome, you have placed the power of God inside my beloved daughter as you have saved us all from these mad minded people. I truly appreciate and respect your kind-ness and mighty power as I'm very glad to see that you are on God's side," King Hemiro said.

"Your majesty, this is the purpose of the God of the Enlightenment," said Krome. "A person who has a good heart and clean soul like Princess Hollidia could learn, improve, and possesses these powers faster as she now becomes the force of the enlightenment to fight against the force of darkness. For Protus, he was a little slower than her because his mind was contaminated by Valimus's and Diron's darkness but he will overcome this shadow."

The king was watching every move of his daughter with the great impression and turned to ask Krome again as he wanted to go down to see them fight on the court.

"Krome, can we go down now? I want to see them closer," the king asked.

"Your majesty, we don't want to distract their con-centrations and besides it is not really safe for you to go down there yet . . . please be patient your majesty," Krome said.

Valimus ordered more soldiers to fight against Princess Hollidia and Protus. Princess Adelia asked Krome to let her help them. Adelia then flew off from the king's room down to the royal court and asked the rest of the soldiers to stay out; otherwise, they would get hurt or die. These were the issues between the royal family, Valimus, and Diron and they did not have to sacrifice their lives for either side.

"I ask all of you do not listen to Valimus and Diron; if you listen to me, you will be safe and be forgiven. This is a matter between the royal family and Valimus. You must let us resolve this problem without your interference." Princess Adelia warned the soldiers.

The soldiers suddenly backed out and they stood to watch Diron and Valimus fight against Protus and Princess Hollidia. Valimus and Diron looked at Princess Adelia with great surprise, as if they had never seen her before.

"Valimus, Diron, you all have betrayed your king and people of Almar Kingdom because you are hungry for power as you have always worshiped the God of Darkness to gain your desires. Today the God of the Enlightenment will judge both of you upon your evil actions against the will of Almar Kingdom," Princess Adelia said.

"Another pretty face . . . you want to taste our power and you have spoken well to stop my soldiers. I will show you my dark powers, which you cannot imagine," Valimus said.

"Princess Hollidia can you take care of Diron, I will face Valimus because he has killed my father and poisoned my mind," Protus said.

"Princess Hollidia . . . I just can't imagine how you

know to fight like this but I still love you as much as I always have," Diron said as he regained his full strength back from the battle with Protus. He really wanted to test Princess Hollidia's power as he was ready for another fight. Valimus looked at Protus and Princess Adelia, as he felt a little bit worried if the two would fight with him at the same time, he would be in real trouble. Princess Adelia looked at Valimus's face and she knew what exactly he had been thinking then she spoke to him with her gentle character.

"Valimus to be fair with you, I will not join Protus to fight against you," said Adelia. "So when you lose, you don't have to feel too bad for the unfairness."

Valimus was very mad inside; he was never looked down on by any woman in battle before. He used his stronger energy to fire the power ball toward her hand as she lifted it to show it to him. Again Adelia continued to tease Valimus while she was holding his dark energy ball in her left hand up in the air.

"That is all you can do, Valimus . . . the promise is the promise . . . when I say I will not fight with you, I definitely will not fight you . . . and here is your ball, take it back and enjoy your game with Protus," Princess Adelia said as she gently threw the energy ball back to Valimus. Adelia transformed his dark energy ball to a very hot one a moment before she threw it back to him. Valimus was so shocked when he took his energy ball back; he felt his whole right arm was burning. He thought he had underestimated her power as he realized that she was the strongest among the three of them. Protus looked at Valimus as he tried to recall what had happened back in Freewill Valley. The moment Valimus slashed his blade at his father's throat and his people pulled his mother away from him.

"Valimus, today you will repay your life for my father's life, my people at Freewill Valley, and the crimes you committed against the king," Protus said.

Valimus held his sword up swinging and slashing at Protus fiercely as he spun his body in the air. Protus blocked Valimus's blade from every direction and learned to absorb the surrounding energies at the same time as Princess Hollidia did. After he learned to control his angers and emotions, Protus had made progression on his skill, energy, and intelligence as fast as Princess Hollidia. Valimus flew like the speed of an arrow and aimed his sword at Protus's chest but Protus flew backward with the same speed of Valimus in the equilibrium of force as the blade was pointing straight at his chest. He withdrew Valimus's dark energy at the same time and converted it into his own energy. Princess Adelia kept watching Protus and Princess Hollidia battled with Valimus and Diron. She could feel Protus's and Princess Hollidia's cosmic energies were improved far better than Diron and Valimus as they learned to control, absorb, dispense, and conserve the amount of their energies.

Diron had tried all his best to defeat Princess Hollidia but his wizard power seemed to have no influence over Princess Hollidia. His constant attacks were getting weaker and he even fought harder than he did with Protus.

"What is wrong with you Diron? Where is your power that you want to show to me? Is it all you can do? I think I can teach you to do better than this," Princess Hollidia asked Diron as she could see his face was getting mad with her fighting capability.

Princess Hollidia knew Diron's strength was weaker and she used her strong energy to strike him back at his chest as she blocked his blade with her royal blade above

167

her face. Diron could feel the pain on his upper chest as he fell back on the ground. Princess Hollidia sent another ball of energy directly to his body as he tried to stand up. Diron fell back on the ground as the sword fell off from his hand and the blood came out of his mouth. He lay down on his back and looked desperately for the soldiers to help him but no one came out to save him as they could see his life was near the end. Princess Hollidia landed a distance in front of him and she spoke with her sweet smile.

"Oh sorry . . . Wizard Diron, for hurting you so bad, but this is not enough for what you have done to my father . . . you have put the spell on him so he became sick then you could poison him with your deadly potion," Princess Hollidia said to Diron as she slowly walked close to him with the sword in her hand.

Diron crawled backward on his back and begged Princess Hollidia for forgiveness and to spare his life.

"Please, Princess Hollidia . . . don't kill me. I've been taking orders from Lord Valimus . . . please spare my life, your highness," Diron begged.

Valimus saw Princess Hollidia finally defeat Diron; he was getting scared as he was getting weaker. Protus understood this was the good time to strike Valimus as he knew his strength and mind were weak. Protus quickly lifted his body, spinning through the air faster than the speed of the arrow toward Valimus with the mighty slash of his blade. Valimus's armor was cutting through as his chest was bleeding, then he fell down on the ground. He got hurt very bad as he was struggling to get up. Princess Adelia told Protus to stop as she knew he would try to finish him off.

"Protus, you must hold on . . . don't kill him now . . . let the king see him first," Adelia said as she flew and landed next to Protus.

Valimus wondered when he heard the king's word in Princess Adelia's conversation. He wanted to get up but he could not because of his wound. Krome told the king this was the time he could go down to see them. King Hemiro ran from his room to the royal court to see his daughter and the rest of the people as Merida followed behind him. Krome appeared on the royal court from nowhere and stood next to Adelia, Protus, and Princess Hollidia. The guards turned around and made way as they saw King Hemiro and Merida walk out of the palace. The king walked to the court and got close to Princess Hollidia and held her shoulder and kissed her head as he spoke to congratulate her and Protus.

"Amazing and congratulations to both of you for defeating the traitors," said the king. "I am very disappointed for the two of you, Valimus and Diron, after I have trusted you with all my heart. You now have betrayed me and want to destroy even my daughter's life and my kingdom. If Krome had not showed up perhaps my life and my whole kingdom would be ruined by the two of you. Now you see the force of darkness never prevails and you both will be judged upon your crimes."

Valimus and Diron knew they would be thrown into the dungeon for the crimes they had committed to overthrow the king. They combined their last powers to throw the dagger at the king's heart but Krome used his cosmic energy to catch both daggers in his hands. With the reaction, Protus and Princess Hollidia threw their swords with their spiritual energies straight through Valimus's and Diron's hearts at the same time and they both died a moment later. King Hemiro turned to thank Krome for saving his life again and ordered the guards to arrest Valimus's knights who volunteered to fight by his side. He ordered the guards to release the good leaders from the prison and throw the soldiers who were loyal to Valimus in the dungeon.

"Krome . . . I owe my life to you twice and thank you for saving my life again. I don't know how I can repay you for your great redemption," King Hemiro said.

"Your majesty, I have never wanted anything more than just to make everyone to be safe and live with peace under the will of the God of the Enlightenment," said Krome, "and my work here is done and soon I will go back to the place where I belong."

Merida was very surprised to hear Krome's conversation with King Hemiro as she thought Krome would stay here with her for the rest of her life.

"Krome, what did you just say? Where are you going, my beloved son? I . . . I want to live by your side until I die," Merida asked Krome.

"Mother, I will visit you from time to time . . . here is not my place . . . I have my own place on this planet and I will always keep my eyes upon this kingdom," Krome answered his mother as he reached out to kiss her forehead. With his power, Merida felt completely calm and happy. She felt so peaceful and her mind was clear from all depression as Krome used his spiritual power to heal his mother's mentality.

15

The Enlightenment

The guards released Prime Minister Deeconus, Lord Tamona, General Valkon, and the rest of the good leaders who were arrested by Valimus. King Hemiro personally apologized for this misunderstanding and rewarded them back their previous jobs and titles. The entire kingdom went back to normal and the soldiers even had more respect and confidence with their king as they saw how powerful Princess Hollidia and Protus were during the battles between Valimus and Diron. Protus was promoted to the Head of Armies and would be the future king. All men served under Protus, obeyed him as Lord Protus, and respected his capability. Princess Hollidia and Protus were awarded with the Medallions of Patriotism as they both fought side by side to save the kingdom. Krome and Adelia were honored by the king as the highest spiritual persons on the entire planet and he asked them to stay in Almar Palace longer to celebrate Protus's and Princess Hollidia's wedding.

"Krome, since you don't accept any rewards from me. . . . I would like to ask you and Princess Adelia to stay here longer to celebrate the new king and his wedding," said King Hemiro. "Besides you should spend more time here with your mother because I've never seen Lady Merida as happy as this for the last ten years."

Krome and Adelia agreed with the king and they wanted to make Merida feel more happy as they wanted to congratulate and celebrate for the new king and his wedding.

"Your majesty, we can stay here longer for your request and I want to make my mother to feel better as we want to help to bring prosperity to this kingdom," Krome said.

Merida was more joyful to hear Krome and Adelia to stay here longer with her; she went to thank King Hemiro for asking them to stay. She also appreciated the king for crowning Protus to be king and the king apologized for letting Valimus kill Optimus.

"Lady Merida . . . I know that I'm getting old and I want Protus to be king as you know your grandfather was once a good king for this nation," said King Hemiro, "and I want to ask you for a pardon for the mistake of letting Valimus kill your husband, Optimus."

"Thank you, King Hemiro . . . I have never been mad with you . . . you've always been kind to my family and you are the good king for this kingdom," Merida said.

Princess Hollidia was more beautiful than ever with her pink and purple dress as she walked along the gardens with Protus and talked about their wedding plans. She turned around and stopped as she had a secret smile as she looked at Protus. She told Protus to close his eyes and she walked close to him then she kissed him on his lips for a moment. Princess Adelia and Krome saw them from a distance and they were really happy to see the couple had lovely lives. Adelia turned to looked at Krome with her beautiful smile as she started to talk about the first time she met him and how she used to feel for him.

"Krome, did you see them? They are a very happy couple as their wedding is near. Do you remember the day

I first met you at the great lake after you killed the giant snake. . . . I've never forgotten that peaceful feeling," said Adelia as she took a deep breath and moved close to Krome. "I did not know how you felt that day but for me, I was very sure to give my life to you. I've never forgotten that moment and I still feel the same way."

Princess Adelia closed her eyes and gave Krome a kiss on his lips. She then opened her eyes and looked straight into his eyes as she continued her conversation with her smile.

"You are still the same Krome as the first day I saw you . . . you have never changed and even you . . . you are always like this . . . and every time I kissed you, I always feel you care and delight inside and your powers made me feel like I'm being touched by an angel. This makes me feel very special," said Adelia as she put her arms around his waist.

"I used to feel odd as I see you have no reaction when I kiss you . . . but now . . . now I understand you through my power that you are different . . . you love me as much as I love you, even though you do not show it . . . but our love is in the higher level beyond cyberian affections. Only you and I would understand this feeling," Adelia said.

Princess Adelia's appearance could be compared to her absolute beauty and she even looked more gorgeous in the pretty light blue and light yellow royal dress that Merida made for her. Krome looked at her innocent pretty face without talking then he reached out to pick one of the beautiful, light pink, rose flowers from the garden along the sidewalk and gave it to Adelia as he started to speak to her.

"Adelia this one is for you . . . you know you are a part of me . . . God brought us together for the reasons, for the purposes of lives and happiness. I'm happy that you are able to understand how I feel," Krome said as he lifted his hands to touch Adelia's face. They then walked toward Princess Hollidia and Protus.

"Congratulations Princess Hollidia, congratulations Protus for your coming wedding. We are happy to see you both will spend your lives together as husband and wife," Adelia said.

"Thank you, Princess Adelia, I will be happy to sit by the side of my future king, King Protus," said Princess Hollidia. "We will have many children when we grow old."

Princess Hollidia turned to look at Krome and she smiled as she spoke to him about his longer stay.

"Thank you, Krome for your longer stay to celebrate our wedding. . . . This will be a great honor for us to have you here and again thank you for the greatest things you have done for all of us here . . . without you, we will not enjoy to see these days," Princess Hollidia said.

"My great pleasure is to help the good people to have peaceful lives and to thank the God of the Enlightenment to give this opportunity to me to serve the will of his destinies," said Krome. "Without him, we all would be perished into the darkness."

"When will you leave, Krome?" Protus asked his brother.

"A few more years we will go back . . . congratulations to both of you to start the new lives together . . . peace, happiness and the enlightenment always be with you and remember to always use your power and wisdom to serve good purposes and the truth. I will have no gifts for both of you on your wedding day. . . . The gifts that I have are only the gifts of the powers, which I've taught and shown it to you . . . with these powers there will be no cyberian can ever harm the two of you. You are a perfect pair just like Adelia and me . . . and as long as you two stay to-gether your powers and health will grow stronger as your lives will thrive and live longer," Krome said.

A few days passed by fast. In Almar Kingdom King Hemiro announced the wedding of Princess Hollidia and Protus as he invited many people in the kingdom to cele-brate his daughter's wedding. Almar citizens wowed the couple as they rode on the wagon along the court in front the king's palace. They were more surprised to see Krome's and Princess Adelia's charms as they rode on an-other wagon behind Protus and Princess Hollidia. The children, the young men and women shouted to them as they were their heroes; Protus and Krome stopped their wagons then they all got off from the wagons and went to shake hands with the children and citizens who greeted them. The two couples were attracted by the crowds be-cause of their charms and beauties with which no one could be compared. They wowed to the appearances of Protus and Princess Hollidia but when they saw Princess Adelia and Krome, they were speechless. Their eyes, hair, skin tones, the shapes of their bodies, the heights and their gentle characters belonged to the angels. That was what the citizens of Almar Kingdom believed and de-scribed. They waved to the crowds as they walked and got back on their wagons.

King Hemiro ordered all his leaders and Wizards to join the wedding of his daughter and then the coronation of Protus to be the king in the same day. The royal ser-vants decorated the stage with colorful flowers, plants and royal furniture and prepared food and drinks for the ceremonies. Musicians performed the royal concert as the two couples arrived at the court. The king gave a speech and then the ceremonies began. Protus and Princess Hollidia were married and blessed by the royal Wizard

175

and the king and Lady Merida. Then the coronation of Protus and Princess Hollidia began as King Hemiro crowned Protus with his monarchial crown and crowned Princess Hollidia with her mother's monarchial crown. All highest Wizards blessed the new king and new queen, then all leaders paid respect to King Protus and Queen Hollidia. The celebrations lasted the whole day and now the new king had arisen to give a speech and to greet the nation.

"Good day to every citizen of Almar Kingdom. First of all, Queen Hollidia and I would like to thank the God of the Enlightenment, the great citizens of Almar Kingdom, my beloved mother, Lady Merida, my beloved father-in law, King Hemiro, my royal leaders, my respectful wizards, and my very special heroes, Krome and Princess Adelia, who are gathering here today to share my blessing life with my beloved wife, Queen Hollidia, and the coronation of the new king. Today is a bright day for all of us and is the day that we celebrate the new way of life as the light of the God of the Enlightenment finally and will forever shine upon our kingdom and our citizens. As your new king, I promise to lead our nation through this new chapter . . . the chapter that every citizen will have a good life and the freedom to live in peace, harmony, happiness and, of course, the respect of the values of the individual idea. This chapter will guarantee our kingdom the security and a safe place for every citizen today, tomorrow, and for many generations to come under the wills of the God of the Enlightenment . . . and these responsibilities begin within each of us. This chapter brings all of us closer together with no corruption, no suppression from any type of the governmental institutions, no hatred among ourselves, no darkness in our hearts and as the children of the bright God, we shall not live our lives in the shadow of darkness and will not allow the dark forces to terrorize our lives and our land. This chapter will surely teach our children and us to choose between right and wrong, good and evil; and will lead us into the bright society with great prosperities on every corner of the kingdom. Krome is our great savior and our hero who has saved us all from the force of darkness and led us into this new chapter; therefore, we shall never forget this greatest gift from our Creator, the God of the Enlightenment. From this chapter on we know where we stand as we clearly see what direction we should take and the choice is clear that we will all follow the God of the Enlightenment, not the darkness for sure. As your king, I promise all the citizens of Almar Kingdom that I will be a good servant to the people and our kingdom . . . and I will lead all of you to defend her from the darkness. Today, the sky is clear and the sun is very bright . . . may this bright day represents our starting point and time . . . and each day will always be a bright day for all of us as we live in the enchanted light to share the happiness, peace, and harmonies among our people. And the powers of the Enlightenment are always with all of us. God bless our kingdom and our people," King Protus gave a speech.

The great sound of applause from all people to greet the new king and queen after Protus gave the great speech from his heart under Krome's guidance. The citizens of Almar shouted to cheer the new king and queen and they thanked Krome and Princess Adelia. Protus was officially and legally king of Almar Kingdom and Princess Hollidia became the new queen of the nation. Lady Merida was crowned as the first lady and King Hemiro demoted himself to the first gentleman as he crowned Protus to be the new king. He wanted to travel around the kingdom and around the planet with Merida. He thought life was too precious and too short so he should enjoy nature and be able to see many different places. He realized that he should leave the king's job to the new king, King Protus.

The whole kingdom became more orderly and there was neither corruption nor suppression as the citizens used to suffer under Valimus's dictatorship. People were happy with the new king as they happily lived with peace without the corruption and pressure from the government or harm from wicked wizards like Diron. Their lives had more freedom and more prosperity as the economics had grown with many new ideas and products across the kingdom. The king ordered the government to build new infrastructures, new water navigation systems, the building code, and the sewer system for the nation as the money flowed in from the taxation of the farms, the industries, and the businesses. The citizens in Almar Kingdom united together to support King Protus and Queen Hollidia to build their nation with new research institutions, universities, hospitals, congregations, and town halls. Almar had become the first nation on the planet with the highest standard of living, highest education, and advanced technologies and it was considered as the cleanest and richest kingdom on the planet. King Hemiro, Lady Merida, Princess Adelia and Krome traveled to every corner of the nation to encourage people to improve their lives with assistance from the king and government as well as the knowledge and beliefs of the God of the Enlightenment.

As the result of hard work from Krome, Princess Adelia, Lady Merida, King Hemiro, King Protus, and Queen Hollidia the progressions and the achievements were succeeded faster than people could imagine. The whole kingdom had only one belief that was the God of the

Enlightenment as people came together to realize this was the right path to lead them to harmony and civilization. The entire kingdom had no crime or hatred as more and more people became honest and fertile citizens. King Hemiro just could not believe his own eyes as he admired Krome for his vision and the will of his power as well as his philosophy. The king had experience with the greatest concepts as he traveled along with Krome from place to place, he became very close to Krome and Princess Adelia and he respected Krome like a true messiah.

"Your majesty, here there are plenty of natural resources to support the entire population and the only things that we need are the idea and the skill to turn these vast soils into the great farms with fruit trees and varieties of crops along this great river. Here people can build a new town with prosperity and it will be easy for them to commute by land or water to the other cities including Almar city," Krome explained to the king as he pointed out the great plain along the Almar River. King Hemiro picked up the soils to see it and he totally agreed with Krome. People had developed many new towns with help from the king and government and with the ideas from Krome and Adelia and even King Hemiro, they enriched their lives with the brand new houses, farms, town halls, shopping centers, schools, and congregations. The king and the government discovered and developed many more mining sites for gold, silver, coal, iron, copper, and even crude oil. Krome showed Almarian people the purpose of life and the knowledge to make things and equipment, which were useful for people. He warned the people not to develop things that could harm the people and the environment of the planet.

Seven years had gone by like seven days for Krome and Adelia; Protus and Princess Hollidia had a son, named Colesus, and a daughter, named Emilia. King Hemiro and Lady Merida were very happy with their grandchildren as well as they saw the whole nation at peace and prosperity. Krome and Adelia were satisfied with their hard works for Almar Kingdom and were happy for King Protus and Queen Hollidia. They knew their works were finished here at Almar and they were ready to leave. Krome told his mother and everybody that Adelia and he would be leaving back to Samatean Kingdom tomorrow.

King Protus and Queen Hollidia ordered the royal servants to prepare the royal banquet to thank Krome and Adelia for their great works and assistances which they had done throughout the kingdom and to say farewell to his brother and Princess Adelia for their journey back to Samatean Kingdom. Many people in the kingdom recognized that Krome and Adelia stayed young as the first day they met them. Krome and Adelia had never told anybody about the existence of the Oradius plant, as they knew this was a secret, which the God of the Enlightenment had forbidden from all the cyberians. Krome had never told Princess Adelia about the secret plant since he met her. Through his supernatural power, she had became one just like him and she comprehended the existence of the Oradius with her supernatural intellectuality during the transformation of their energies.

On the next day in the late morning Krome and Princess Adelia got on horseback after he informed his family, the king and queen of Almar Kingdom to go back to the Samatean Kingdom to visit Adelia's parents. King Hemiro and Lady Merida asked Krome and Adelia if they could come along to visit the Samatean Kingdom, especially Adelia's parents. Krome and Adelia agreed to bring them along to see different country, besides King Hemiro wanted to meet Adelia's father for the second time after his first visit thirty years ago when the two kingdoms had become allies. King Protus and Queen Hollidia wished they could come along to visit Adelia's kingdom but they had great responsibilities to take care of their kingdom.

Protus gave one great white horse to Krome as a gift for his brother. Krome accepted the gift from his brother and he thought it would be a good companion to Adelia's horse. Protus sent a message to the king and queen of Samatean to inform them of King Hemiro's visit. He also sent a big ship with twenty of the best knights to guard his mother and King Hemiro on their trip to visit Samatean Kingdom. King Protus, Queen Hollidia, and the children waved their hands in farewell good-byes.

"We never say good-bye in our other world . . . we will be always with all of you," said Krome. "Please may the power of the Enlightenment be with all of you . . . and remember the will of the God of the Enlightenment."

Krome and Princess Adelia rode on the white horses along with the royal wagon and the guards toward the Almar shore. Across the ocean, Princess Adelia and Krome enjoyed their ride back to the Samatean Kingdom as well as Lady Merida and King Hemiro. Not for long they had arrived at the Samatean Kingdom and they were welcomed by Princess Adelia's parents' hospitalities. Adelia's parents were very excited to see her as her mother embraced her in front of everyone. Adelia turned around to introduce King Hemiro and Lady Merida to her parents.

"Father, I would like to introduce these people to you. This is King Hemiro, the previous king of Almar Kingdom. Here is Lady Merida and she is Krome's mother. Of course you have not probably forgotten Krome, my guardian angel," Adelia said.

"Welcome to my kingdom King Hemiro, Lady Merida, Krome, my greatest hero, and everyone else. This is very great opportunity for me to show my humble gratitude to the greatest warrior, Krome. I really apologize for my blindness under Mongon's dark power that he had planned to destroy you and my daughter. You have saved my daughter from the snake and again from Mongon. And beyond that you have saved my whole kingdom, my family, and my people. Please . . . please forgive my mistake and misunderstanding that I had done to you and Adelia," Adelia's father said.

"Your majesty, please stand up . . . I had seen all Mongon's actions and the wills of the God of Darkness. For your majesty, I have neither madness nor hatred toward your act of misunderstanding but I am very happy to see that now you have led your people into the prosperities and the wills of the God of the Enlightenment. I see quite a change in this entire kingdom in the last seven years . . . I know that you have been following the will of the right God and the Samatean people are moving in the right direction," Krome said.

Krome lifted Adelia's father's arms to stand up as he tried to kneel down before him to ask for the forgiveness of his wrong doing in the past. Krome knew that Adelia's father had completely changed after Adelia killed Mongon and the bad leaders seven years ago. Most of the leaders and the soldiers, who had served her father's kingdom, were very loyal and honest to the kingdom. The citizens of Samatean were very happy and amazed to see Princess Adelia and Krome return to Samatean. They came to greet them with high respect as Adelia's great legend had spread all over the kingdom seven years ago. They could not believe their own eyes when they saw her absolute beauty and her ageless youth. Most of them believed that Adelia had turned into an angel because of her pure love and the sacrifice, which she was willing to make just to save the people in her kingdom. King Hemiro and Lady Merida were even more joyful to see that the God of the Enlightenment blessed Samatean Kingdom and its citizens.

"It is the greatest honor and pleasure to see you and your queen again, King El Candor. You have transformed your country into a very modern place on this planet and your people really live in the prosperity and happiness. . . . I truly admire your kingship and your envision of the Enlightenment," King Hemiro said.

"Thank you, King Hemiro . . . this is the work of Krome, which he has brought to your kingdom but his work also taught me and my people here too as in these past seven years my Ambassadors kept sending me all the good news in Almar Kingdom . . . I have asked my people to do the same in our kingdom. I really want to visit Almar Kingdom as I have heard that your new king and your people have transformed the whole country into the most modern society on this planet. Here we still need to make improvement on every corner of the kingdom. I have heard that now you are retired from your throne. I wish that I could do the same thing . . . but there is no one to replace my position. I think I'm not really lucky like you. Hah, hah, hah," King El Candor said. "I think Krome will not be interested to be the king . . . and neither Adelia would like to be the queen to rule this kingdom. Perhaps I will wait until my long lost distant nephew is old enough or someone else who will be qualified to take my place."

"Your majesty, I hope that you will find someone, very special, to take your place then you can go around to see different places like us. We have been enjoying lives outside the royal palace for a long time and we truly love it," Lady Merida said.

"Um . . . you are complete right, Lady Merida, as I can see your youthfulness is getting younger and the look on King Hemiro's face. This even is making me to be more jealous with both of you that life has not been so fair for both of us," King El Candor said.

"Queen Amelida, I'm very thrilled to have Princess Adelia by the side of my son, Krome, and I'm very pleased that we finally have met. God has blessed us all to see this day. I think she is absolutely beautiful," Lady Merida said.

"Yes, Lady Merida, I'm completely speechless when I see my beloved daughter is back to our kingdom. Krome and Adelia are truly born to be a perfect pair under the will of the God of the Enlightenment. Her beauty has totally changed and now she possesses an angel's appearance. I appreciate that Krome has saved her from the darkness again and again. Her life is fulfilled when she is by your son's side . . . and I feel like I have been touched by the angels," Adelia's mother said.

King El Candor had ordered the whole kingdom to celebrate to welcome Krome, Princess Adelia, King Hemiro, and Lady Merida. He and King Protus had signed the permanent relationship, trade, and laws of the two countries as one country and will allow the citizens of the two countries to hold both citizenships and will protect each other in wartime. That night at Samatean palace, the great fireworks lit up in the sky as the sound of music and dances were performed in the royal feast to celebrate the victory of the God of the Enlightenment over the God of the Darkness. Krome and Adelia held each other and stood on the balcony and looked at the happiness upon people's faces.

"This is the kind of life that God wants us to live with . . . I think tomorrow we will go back to Aquarium Mountain, the place that we really belong, Adelia," Krome said.

"Yes, Krome . . . it is definite." Adelia answered as she gave Krome a sweet kiss.

Thus, Krome and Adelia sat on the top of Aquarium Mountain for many million years to protect the secret plant and defend the whole planet from the God of the Darkness. Often they flew down to different places just to save and protect people from the dark forces as they showed them how to live better lives, which was called the Enlightenment.